# FULL
# CIRCLE

## A FAMILY'S JOURNEY TO FREEDOM

LUCY BELLA DONNA

FULL CIRCLE

Published by
Scribblers Press
9741 SE 174th Place Road
Summerfield, Florida 34491

Printed by
Trinity Press
3190 Reps Miller Road, Suite 360
Norcross, Georgia 30071

Library of Congress Control Number: 2023907286
Lucy Bella Donna, 04/18/2023

FULL CIRCLE - Lucy Bella Donna

**Summary:** This story is a work of fiction. The characters, events, places, entities, and names were imagined and created by the author for fiction. Any resemblance to persons living or dead is coincidental. Any scenes depicted in a court of law is imagined by the author to add drama to the story and may not necessarily take place in a courtroom.

Authentic places, locations, known names, and entities were mentioned to give a sense of reality to the story.

Paperback:  ISBN: 978-1-950308-56-9
Kindle: 978-1-950308-62-0

# DEDICATION

I dedicate this book, Full Circle, to my nephew who entered God's kingdom on April 6, 2021, Donald Francis Farina. Donald was my Godchild.

I pray this story will touch the hearts of those searching for answers. It is God's promise that if you seek Him, you will find Him. Donald did!

I would also like to mention my children and their spouses who have supported me in telling my stories: to Paul, to Lisa and Eric, to Jennifer and John, and to Tommy and Amy, I say Thank You.

To my grandchildren, Alyssa, Hannah, Sarah, and Leah, you have been such a light in my life.

A special thank you to my nephew, Michael Farina, and his daughter, Gianna, and to my niece, Christine, and her husband, Todd Lawson. Thank you for the love and support you have given your parents, Cathy and Don, during a difficult time.

May the Lord bless you all, with His peace and comfort.

# ACKNOWLEDGEMENTS

I would like to give a special thank you to our publisher, Charles De Andrade, author of many books, including the Steward Series. He is the founder of Scribblers Press Publishing, as well as Scribblers writing groups, and the Scribblers Online Book Store.

Thank you Charles, for your suggestions and your help in formatting my story and for encouraging the writers to use our life's experiences and incorporate them into our narratives.

I would also like to acknowledge the Scribblers who have encouraged me to go on with my project. I thank them for their suggestions to help make my story resonate with the readers.

A special thank you to Trinity Press and to Graphic Designer, Bridgett Joyce. Her creative design skills have turned my idea into a reality, seeing that my project reach its goal.

I extend my gratitude to Jennifer Miller Siegel, author of Love for Harrison. Thank you Jenn, for your help and encouragement during the process of writing your own story, one that has turned a tragedy into a triumph!

Finally, I wish to thank Pat Peoples Smith, author of Snowball Investing, for her insight on which book cover would best suit my story. Thank you, Pat!

## About our Editor

I would like to send my gratitude to Dr. Randi D. Ward, for her time, encouragement, and editing skills. Dr. Ward is an Award Winning Author and teacher of English Literature. She is the recipient of many awards, including the IAOTP Award 2019, for top female Entrepreneur and Empowered Woman, and the top IAOTP Female Visionary and Lifetime Achievement Award, of 2021.

Dr. Ward has been featured in current magazines, anthologies, and radio/video programs, as well as documentaries, and is currently Editor in Chief of Inspirations for Better Living, Morocco Pens, CMR Unlimited, and LOANI. She has received the Woman of the Year award, in both writing and language arts.

Dr. Randi D. Ward is well traveled, having visited 60 countries around the globe, and has previously owned two English language schools in Cairo, Egypt, where she taught there during the 2011-2012 revolution.

In 2020, Dr. Randi D. Ward received the "She Inspires Me Award," and the SIMA "Special Love Award," which doesn't surprise me. There are many more awards I could mention, but to me, Dr. Randi D. Ward is known for her compassion and love for others, and that's the ultimate award anyone can achieve.

Dr. Randi D. Ward, 2020 Educator of the Decade by IAOTP, International #1 Best Selling Author, Visionary Book Writing Coach and Master Editor, International Speaker, and Humanitarian.

*Full Circle* is a powerful story about a family and its interaction with each other and with those in the community in which the family resides. It embraces family and religious values. It demonstrates the power of believing in God and following His plan. The author beautifully depicts her characters and settings to make the readers feel and sympathize with their situations and problems and learn from their mistakes as well. As the editor of this delightful, inspiring book, I was privileged to be one of the first people to read this overall, well written story. I highly recommend this book to all readers from teenagers to adults. Important life lessons will be learned.

"ALL THAT THE FATHER GIVETH ME SHALL COME TO ME; AND HIM THAT COMETH TO ME I WILL IN NO WISE CAST OUT." (JOHN 6:37 KJV)

# TABLE OF CONTENTS

# TABLE OF CONTENTS (continued)

# INTRODUCTION

Born into a poor family in Hong Kong, Chen Young had visions of migrating to America. With aspirations of attending college, followed by the police academy, he would become a hero of sorts, defending the vulnerable victims he encountered in his town. He would be highly respected by its citizens. But the enticements of the world called his name, and Chen Young got caught up in the underworld. He liked the perks. That is, until he met his wife, Niki, and was presented with a way out of his lifestyle. The story of his transformation, and his redemption, can be found in the book The Ledger, A Story of Redemption, by Lucy Bella Donna.

Full Circle will take you back thirty years, from the story's present day, to Hong Kong and to Chen Young's childhood. Li and Hua Young are struggling to survive, working long hours in a sweat shop, in order to put food on the table. Living in a walk-up, low-rise, near the Quarry Bay, Li and Hua are facing an unknown future as Li Young is accused of working for the black market in Hong Kong. He awaits his trial in a Kowloon prison.

The story opens with Chen Young, now a grown man, pastoring a small New England church that is nestled in the foothills of the Green Mountains. Learning day by day how to assist in meeting the needs of his congregants, he discovers the importance of trusting the Lord. How do you help a learning disabled child who is harassed every day and bullied at school? How do you advise a young teenage girl who is raped, yet she wants to keep her baby? Sadly, these are some of the problems facing the teenage world today. The characters will learn, as time goes on, there *is* an answer.

As the story nears its ending, Li Young is swept up into the world of fashion, with the choice of starting his own clothing line. Will he accept the offer, or will he return to his quiet life in the foothills? We all have choices we must make in life, decisions that will change the direction of our lives forever. For Li Young the choice is easy. Chen Young will struggle to find his peace.

From civil servant to criminal, from criminal to Christian, from Christian to pastor, you can find Chen's story and his family's story in The Ledger, A Story of Redemption and in Full Circle, A Family's Journey to Freedom.

## FULL CIRCLE

## CHAPTER ONE
### (Parsonage Life - Mid-1990s)

The old church had lived up to its age. It was built with quarry stones, gray ones, of different shapes and sizes that sparkled like precious gems when kissed by the sun. They were covered in plaster made of gypsum, a mineral more costly than the common sand or lime minerals used in constructing dry walls and interiors, but it took less time to set. It was favored by carpenters and sculptors alike.

There were stained glass windows on each side of the sanctuary. They were framed in the same type of soft plaster that transformed them into a pointed arch with a cross at the top; Their lacy design resembled the delicate filigree of French artists.

Thin charcoal colored soldering winded around the colored glass sections like a road map, holding each panel in place. The windows depicted various scenes from the Bible; Some were parables. They had the touch of a master.

~~~

Pastor Chen Young had been cleaning the sanctuary. There was a storeroom to the right of the entrance hall that kept boxes of hymnals. The song books were to be placed in the wooden racks attached to the back of each bench after the benches were refurbished. Chen stepped into the closet and lifted a box and brought it into the sanctuary. He placed the carton on one of the benches in the back of the church. He sat and opened it. He drew out one of the hymnals, its hard green cover worn with time. As he opened to the first pages, he thought back to his Christian friends in Hong Kong and how they used to sing hymns in church. He would accompany them on occasion, "just for the heck of it," never thinking one day he would convert to Christianity. "Never!" He smiled.

Chen went through the pages as if his fingertips were dipped in velvet. He treated each page as a delicate flower. He read the printed words that told of the awesome wonder of the Savior, in verse, repeating them one by one: Wonderful, Beautiful, Prince of Peace, Lilly of the Valley, and Gentle Savior. Yet, as a warrior, to return as promised to make all things new, He was Mighty God, King of Kings, Lord of Lords, Great High Priest, and the Lion of Judah.

Chen sat there for at least an hour leafing through the pages as if he had stumbled on a wonderful secret; a hidden treasure that could not be consumed by moths or rust. These old hymns told of the wonders of heaven.

As he closed the book, Chen gazed at the choir loft above the sanctuary entrance where an old pipe organ took up space. The organ was crafted in mahogany, its patina burnished by the years. Its pipes were made of lead, tin, and copper and they were covered in a thick layer of tarnish. As his eyes focused on the old pipes, he imagined how shiny they were before time interfered. He thought of the wonderful sounds they must have created, sounds that resonated through the sanctuary on Sunday mornings, and he thought of the songs of worship that rang out from this small space, the harmony permeating the room and blessing hundreds of past generations. One of his projects would be to restore the pipes to their original shine.

On a sunny day, the color of ripened apricots would cast a tangerine glow to the alcove.

There was a rounded window of stained glass that hung above the organ. It depicted the resurrection of Christ, accompanied by angels. Its golden rays of heavenly light shone down on the Savior, welcoming His return to the

Father. Mission accomplished! "It is finished," Jesus had cried out.

The staircase leading to the loft was made of white pine, brought in from the saw mills of Maine. It was thought to be stronger than the other pines the local wood mills offered. It was graceful in its design, winding its way to the upper level in gentle curves. A black wrought iron railing had been added on years later.

On any given day, from inside the sanctuary, the rays of the sun would penetrate the windows glass panels as an x-ray penetrates the body, casting glows over the old wooden benches of oak: glows of amber, magenta, blue, and emerald, but not on this day. It was dark, and dreary, and cold inside.

~~~

It was early afternoon, when Chen descended the steps to the basement of the old structure to check the heating system. It had rained that morning, and he noticed there were slow drips coming from several openings in the ceiling. He grabbed a few rusted pots that were stacked in a cupboard at the back of the cellar. He placed each one under a leak, hoping he would be back from town before they overflowed. He would pick up a few supplies there. Before he left, he phoned a roofer who promised to be there in the morning.

Chen wondered how much it would cost to finish the repairs the church needed. There was plumbing to be updated, and the electrical system and old boiler needed to be serviced. Chen trusted God would provide. He had to trust. The nest egg he and Niki had saved before moving in would hold them but only for a time.

~~~

The parsonage was an addition to the church, an annex that was added to the back of the building at the turn of the 20th century. It consisted of four rooms on the lower floor and three bedrooms located on the upper level. A bathroom was situated close to the bedrooms. Its walls were covered in pink diamond shaped tiles, trimmed in black. Under a window stood a four-footed soaking tub, a modern look in its day.

The kitchen downstairs was large. It had two sinks that sat side by side. One basin for washing and one for rinsing. Niki Young, the pastor's wife, thought it would be a great place to wash vegetables.

The stove was fueled by gas and the oven large enough to cook a three-course meal. A used washer and dryer stood in the back entrance foyer. Today the foyer would be called a mudroom, a convenient area to leave your snow boots in the winter and wet umbrellas, bathing suits, and fishing gear in the summer.

There was a cold cellar below the upper floors made of concrete blocks. It was a perfect place for storing food items. Niki intended to make full use of it.

The parsonage had casement windows that cranked open and a large potbelly stove that sat in one corner of the living area. The couple thought the stove added an old-world charm. For Niki and ChenYoung their home was ideal.

~~~

Reverend Chen Young was short in stature, with small dark eyes, shiny black hair and teeth as white as eggshells. In his younger days he would wear his hair long and tied back in a pony tail. Now, as a pastor, he decided to shorten it. Either way, it was always shiny.

Chen had a quick pace when he walked, like a man who was sure of himself and knew where he was going, unlike his father who was timid and shy. He must have inherited his mother's genes, he surmised. His personality had endeared his wife, Niki, to him. He often asked himself why. Why had she stuck with him until his conversion?

Chen had juggled his job as a detective for the Camwood Police Dept., working days and attending school at night. During the summer months, he doubled up on his classes and had received his Bachelor Degree in Criminal Justice. After his conversion to Christianity, he attended a nearby bible college and majored in Theology and Pastoral Studies. He received his Masters Degree from the school of divinity of his choice.

It hadn't been easy for Chen as he tracked down criminals during the day and studied God's word at night, but he knew one day he would help those in trouble—those who had never heard the gospel perhaps and needed someone to show them the way. He remembered the apostle Paul's words to press toward the mark of his calling. He had reached his goal. It was God ordained.

~~~

It was nearing sunset, when Chen left the town to drive home. A rainstorm had been predicted for later that evening. He decided to take a detour and enjoy the countryside. He opened the window of the car and allowed the cool afternoon air to fill his lungs. He took in the landscape around him; its meadows abundant with colorful wildflowers. Sheep could be seen grazing across the hillsides, from one farm to the next, spread out like white wool rugs. In the far distance he could see street lamps illuminating the main roadway. He thought they resembled colonies of fireflies lighting his way home.

For a moment Chen's mind retreated to his new life as a pastor. Would his sermons touch someone, anyone who was willing to listen? If only he had the same faith in himself that his wife had in him. But this was all new to him. He had put effort into his first sermon and hoped the congregants he expected would somehow relate to his interpretation of God's Word. He had scheduled his first service for the following month and prayed word of mouth would follow, drawing in new congregants.

~~~

A light shower had morphed into a downpour. Niki hurried to the kitchen to shut the casement windows. She had gathered some kindling wood, the day before, in the woodlands behind the parsonage and wrapped the damp wood in old towels she had found in the linen closet. She rolled them tight to soak up any moisture left from the elements, then unrolled them and placed the wood on the kitchen counter to dry.

Niki went to the stove in the corner of the living area and opened the flue. She gathered up old newspaper and placed it in the bottom of the old potbelly. Adding kindling wood on top, she lit a small fire. She leaned into the metal bin and chose a large log and placed it on top of the flames. Niki watched as it glowed, lighting and heating the dark room. Once the fire was lit, she added a pile of coals that were stored in the coal bin behind the stove.

Niki filled the kettle with cold water and returned to check on the fire. She placed the kettle on the stove and retreated to the kitchen. She would wait for the water to boil.

Niki opened the cupboard. She took out an old wrought iron trivet and placed it on the table. She sat on the vintage bench left by the previous pastor, who had hoped the couple would find a place for it. She stared at the worn black and white tiles of the flooring and started to doze. The move to the parsonage had taken its toll. She dozed until she heard the kettle whistle.

~~~

Niki was a petite woman with plum colored eyes. Her auburn hair rested on her shoulders in gentle waves. She had worked as a paralegal for many years and continued to work until Chen became ordained. At times, she missed her job, but this was where she needed to be. It was God ordained.

~~~

Chen pulled into the driveway and parked the tan Toyota next to an old willow tree that had stood in the side yard for nearly a century. It reminded him of his younger days in Hong Kong. His grandmother would pack lunches for him and his friends, and they would sit under a weeping cherry tree, its cascading branches providing shelter from the heat or rain, like the arms of a protective parent. Cars and rickshaws would pass by, their passengers unaware there was a group of hungry boys under the tree. The memory brought a smile to his face.

Chen stepped out of the car and lifted its trunk. It contained several packages of hardware that he would need for church repairs and a covered tray containing a complete meal for two. He smiled as he walked into the kitchen and surprised Niki with dinner. Not having to cook, she was grateful for the extra time. "I'll heat it up, it'll only take a few minutes." she said. She kissed him on the cheek and turned the oven on.

After dinner, Niki entered the study with two cups of steaming tea and a plate with cookies she had baked earlier. The couple ate dessert and talked about the time it would take to get things to run smoothly, "like a well-oiled machine," Chen said.

Niki returned to the living area to douse the coals that illuminated the brick hearth. She decided to call it a night.

As she lay in bed, the relentless rain pelted against the casement windows, reminding Niki of the many ceiling leaks that needed fixing. The moon shifted to reveal a black sky. She fell into a deep slumber.

~~~

Chen sat back in his green leather chair. He closed his eyes and thought of the days that brought him to this point in his life. His vision was clear and nostalgic. He reminisced about his youth in Hong Kong, his migration to the States, and how he longed to bring his parents to join him.

As he caught up with his paperwork Chen read a few welcoming letters and paid the first of his monthly bills. He continued to work on his sermon, well into the night. The dimly lit room hurt his eyes, and the Tiffany style lamp flickering on his desk didn't help. He checked its wire and saw it needed to be replaced. He left himself a mental note to return to the hardware store in the morning. It would be an easy fix.

It was after one a.m. when Chen stopped writing. He walked to the door and closed the overhead light. As he stood in the doorway, he turned for one last look. His eyes scanned the room. It was a small room, maybe 12x18 feet. Two long casement windows hung above his mahogany desk. On the opposite wall was a utility closet that was deemed the Lost and Found.

Chen and Niki had agreed, if they could not afford to panel the study, they would make it look as cozy as possible. Its color would be a cappuccino brown. With its blue and beige squares, the cotton print curtains that hung on each side of the casements added the final touch. His study became the inviting and peaceful room they had envisioned. It was the room where he prayed his sermons would come to life.

## CHAPTER TWO
### (Hong Kong 1960s)

The Hong Kong sun would not reveal itself through the angry clouds. A tropical depression had formed in the South China Sea. It was June of 1960. It would take a few days for the storm to travel northward and morph into a typhoon. Fourteen inches of rain covered the island. The wind gusts were forceful and the landslides so great, thousands became homeless. The infrastructure of the colony was destroyed and would need to be rebuilt.

The people of Hong Kong were resilient. In the years that followed they bounced back, causing the city to thrive. The city grew in population and would soon emerge as a major center of finance and culture. The landscape was now one of steel.

Low-rise buildings were replaced by high risers, yet many people remained in the poorer areas working long hours in the textile or garment factories on the island or on the Kowloon peninsula.

Factories sprung up like weeds in springtime. Hong Kong fashion was in demand, becoming popular throughout the world. Famous designers took notice and traveled to the island often to make deals. Luxurious fabrics of silk and embroidery were imported from India and used to make expensive clothing for the rich and for well-known celebrities. Hong Kong had made its mark on societies around the globe.

~~~

Li Young, and his wife Hua, ("your name means flower," her mother had told her,) migrated to Hong Kong in the winter of 1966 when the Cultural Revolution in China had already begun. It was the Chinese year of the fire horse. That previous spring, hoping to reassert his authority over communist rule, the leader of the country had called for an uprising of the younger generation. Li and Hua felt the tension, it was a red flag to them, and they decided to flee the mainland.

~~~

Li was a small man, almost frail, with dark eyes as small as the black seeds of the dragon fruit brought in from the mainland every summer.

His cheeks were wide, and his nose was small and round. His hair was black with a few strands of gray popping up here and there. He continued to dress in traditional Asian clothing; he wore his trousers short and his shirts of solid colors long. Hua preferred a more modern style, colorful, yet simple. Neither had the money to keep up with fashion.

Hua was a tad taller than her husband and wore the customary flat shoes with a thin leather strap across the front. She joked she had shot two hawks with one arrow. The shoes served their purpose. They were almost equal in height. She was neither heavy set, nor was she slim, but of a medium build with dark hair and large dark eyes that resembled black pearls. She had a strong countenance, unlike Li who could not hide his timidity. Hua was in control of the Young family.

~~~

The couple arrived in Hong Kong in late December and settled in a low-rise, walk-up apartment, not too far from Quarry Bay. They obtained work as sewers in a clothing factory, located on the Kowloon Peninsula.

Li was an excellent suit tailor, but he had been assigned to sew men's shirts. Hua was a seamstress. Life was simple: work, home, rest and work again, with one day off— alternating on weekends. The work hours were long, with two short breaks and a longer break in-between for lunch.

Li worked the morning shift. It began at 6 a.m. Hua chose the late afternoon shift, taking a part time position. This would give her time to prepare Li's meals. She would take a later ferry back to Hong Kong Island after her shift ended.

~~~

Li and Hua had met at a textile factory in Beijing, China. Li loved his wife but rarely showed his emotions. Hua, on the other hand, had a warm, gentle nature. She tried her best to see others around her were happy. It wasn't that Li was uncaring. He cared a great deal although he never showed it. He had a way of avoiding tough situations with his daydreaming. It was his way of escape.

As soon as the couple arrived in Hong Kong, they spoke about starting a family. In March of 1967 Hua became pregnant. She was due the following winter. Her mother, Jing, who lived nearby, agreed to help care for the baby; Hua could continue to work.

Jing lived about a mile from the couple's apartment and enjoyed her independence. She had been widowed for five years. She had black hair and black eyes and wore her hair in a Chignon. She was short in stature and unfriendly but helpful to the young couple who needed her.

Li and Hua were happy and found no reason to complain. They had little, but they were grateful to live in a safer environment, having missed the Star Ferry riots that had erupted in Kowloon the previous spring.

~~~

During the previous spring, the British colonial government ruled over Hong Kong and had decided to raise the prices of the passenger harbor crossing from Quarry Bay to the Kowloon Peninsula. Many worked on the peninsula and could not afford the rise in price. The demonstrations were peaceful at first but ended in violence and chaos. Fires were set and rocks thrown, causing destruction. Many were injured, others arrested, and some died. The riots lasted three nights, but months of unrest followed.

## CHAPTER THREE
### (Life in Hong Kong)

The year was 1967. The meteorologist had predicted weather in the high sixties. Li Young shut his alarm and jumped into the shower. He had little time to spare. His breakfast was a quick one, some left over noodles from the night before and a slice of luncheon meat. He filled his thermos with hot tea and grabbed his lunch pail and wallet as he walked out the door. The sun was to rise at six forty-four a.m. He found his way to the train station in the darkness.

Every work day was the same. Li took the train several stops to the Quarry Bay pier and hopped on the Star Ferry to Kowloon to begin his long shift. He chose an outside seat on the top deck, so he could enjoy a view of the harbor. He would watch the activities of the early risers until the coastline slowly disappeared and the people looked like garden ants crawling about.

The sampans that hugged the shore could be seen in uneven rows, bobbing like corks on the choppy water. They were occupied by traders and merchants, all shouting to make a sale. Some slept in them—others went home.

Many merchants rose early, before sunrise. They wanted to catch the early risers, tourists and those who had business on the island, enticing them to buy whatever they had to offer. Hawkers barked, some sang, but all had the same goal—to earn a living.

The fisherman could be seen pushing long poles with paddles in the water, moving their boats in and out of the bay. On hot days the sun would beat down on the waves, transforming them into glistening crystals while sea gulls flew overhead circling the sky, hoping to grab a meal.

On windy days Li loved to watch the men with larger boats as they hoisted their weatherworn canvas sails that fought the wind and guided them into the open waters.

Rickshaws dotted the streets of Hong Kong, their carriers pulling tourists through the winding alleys. The red carriages were contrasted by their gray tarpaulin coverings overhead that protected its riders should the weather turn to rain. Many pullers dressed in lightweight cotton shirts and pants that stopped at their ankles, the dark colors matching the overhangs of their carriages. Shorts were worn on hotter days. Their hats, some with peaks, were made of straw or bamboo and protected them from the rain or the hot sun.

On his day off Li Young would go to the markets with Hua or meet an old friend and fish for Japanese Mackerel or Grouper. Catching a fish or two would be one less meal to buy at the market. The men would take the ferry, their fishing poles and gear in tow, cross past Victoria Harbor and fish when they reached Kowloon side of the bay. Li felt he had a good chance of making a few strikes on that side.

~~~

The couple's low-rise apartment was located near the coastline, not far from Quarry Bay Park. It consisted of two rooms and a small kitchen area. There was a bathroom at the end of a hallway that had a toilet, a shower, and a sink. The tiles were plain white without trim, and the floor tiles were larger squares of white ceramic. Li would feel the cold tiles beneath his feet, especially during the rainy season, and he always wore warm socks when walking about the apartment. Hua couldn't have cared less. The cold never affected her as it did her husband. She would walk barefoot about the apartment when she was home from work. She often teased him about her blood being thicker than his; a trait she inherited from her ancestors, she would say.

The kitchen area was not partitioned off. The neighbors on the floor above did not have to guess what the Youngs were having for dinner. Along with the steam it created, the scent of ginger juice, garlic paste, cooking wine, spring onions or sesame oil, simmering in large pots, would sneak out into the hallway and creep up the stairs to the next level. No one ever complained when Hua was cooking.

The Youngs were simple people with humble beginnings. They came from a line of poor factory workers on the mainland. Their fathers and grandfathers before them worked in the textile industry, producing cotton yarn until the depression of the 1930's hit. After the second Sino-Japanese war, in the late thirties, the mills were destroyed. There was little work. The people remained poor and were resigned to it.

~~~

After they married, Li and Hua expected little from life, except to pay their bills and survive. When their son came along, their focus changed. They wanted better for him. If it took a lifetime, they would send their son to the United States. They felt he would have the opportunity for a better future in America.

Chen Young was born on December l, 1967, in Hong Kong Hospital. Although the Youngs knew raising a child would be hard financially, they welcomed their son and were grateful for his life.

## CHAPTER FOUR
### (Kowloon -The Meeting)

In 1968 the conditions at the Kowloon factory were under code. The workers were used to them and stopped complaining. Lighting was poor, and the seating was so close together, if the workers stretched their arms out they could touch each other. The days were longer than the longest day in summer, and the pay was little. Most factories functioned with three separate shifts, this one had two.

The machines the sewers worked on were industrial ones. Their chassis were made of metal, covered in plastic, and they were built to endure heavier fabrics. They were considered top of the line with zig-zag and embroidery features and foot pedals.

Many types of clothing were made at the Kowloon factory. The styles varied from evening gowns and beaded cardigans to skirts and denim jackets. Designer bags and shoes were also manufactured there.

Li Young worked in the clothing section, making dress shirts with high collars to be worn with ties by wealthy business men and white-collar workers. He was meticulous in his sewing and rarely looked up from his workstation, except when taking a short break or going outside to eat lunch.

~~~

The morning was cold. Li chose to wear his heavier jacket as he dashed out the door. He did not want to miss a moment of the meeting Manager Wang Wei announced would take place. He rode the train to the Quarry Bay Pier and hopped on the Star Ferry to the Kowloon Peninsula. In the darkness he could see silvery vapor hovering over the clouds that had now turned a dark gray. They moved swiftly through the sky, as if they were angry and about to erupt. They would prevent the sun from making its morning debut. The wind brushed across his face as he glanced out over the horizon. It tousled his hair and he felt its freshness.

Li arrived at his job with time to spare. He went to his workstation and placed his jacket over his work chair. He opened his tool box and checked its contents. He would need a certain amount of extra fine silk pins, machine needles— in case one breaks, steel straight pins, and sewing needles. He also kept extra bobbins on hand and several guides for hems and seams. There were attachments for embroidery and certain stitches, but the ones used most often were for making buttonholes. He was never without his tape measure and tailor's chalk which he kept in the top drawer of his workstation.

Everything seemed to be in order. It was not unusual to see Li Young with a flexible yellow tape measure placed around his neck as a doctor would hang his stethoscope.

The sewers section was large, the size of a convention hall. It housed hundreds of workers. It was the morning shift, and the room was usually filled with chatter until the work bell sounded. On this day, there was no time for small talk.

A meeting had not been called in months, and the air was filled with tension, like a traveler caught in a traffic jam, trying to catch a 9 a.m. flight. The silence that followed was deafening.

Manager Wang Wei entered the double doors and walked to the front of the massive room. He was a quiet man, his demeanor subdued. The workers at the factory thought him to be shy and unsure of himself. The fact was he knew exactly what he was doing. He wore loose beige trousers, a black woven cloth belt, a white starched shirt, and a tightly woven black and gray plaid cap with a black leather peak. He never took his hat off, no matter what the season, and most of his staff suspected he was hiding his baldness. Besides his head, he kept his age underwraps, and the only clue to it were his gray eyebrows.

Wang stepped onto the podium, the same podium from which he announced holiday gatherings, factory functions, and local festivals. He had a microphone in his right hand and raised it to his mouth. A shrill went through the room, as he tapped on the microphone several times and tested the equipment. The shrill was like a nail scraping across a slate board; everyone in the room winced.

"One, two, three…may I have your attention please," Wang shouted.

The work bell sounded at exactly 6 a.m. It vibrated, reaching the ears of every cutter, sewer, steam presser, and inspector at the factory.

Wang Wei began to speak in his native language. His voice quaked as he gave his message in Cantonese and repeated it in English: "Kowloon workers, some of you have been with this company for many years. You are able to make a good living, and we have treated you with kindness and respect. We have recently had a violation at our factory, and we must find the person responsible for this outrage and breach of contract that has dishonored us. We will not stop until we find the guilty party. He will be prosecuted to the highest degree."

Wang Wei's eyes were glazed and his shoulders dropped. He went on to say, "Large amounts of our highest quality fabric have been stolen. It is a fabric we have not used before. It was imported from India and made of a pure blue silk. There are twenty rolls missing." Gasps could be heard throughout the room.

Li could barely work. He was shaken and afraid he would be targeted. Several workers had given him a hard time about his having extra fabric to work with. The fact was the workers that accused him were incompetent and made so many sewing errors, they had to use an excess amount of fabric to cover their many mistakes.

The shirts were made with breast pockets—something that required skill. Li rarely made a sewing error and always had fabric left over. Some workers would harass him for extra material. When he gave in, he was barely able to make his quota. Li had had enough.

One sewer, Chang Chao, approached him often for extra fabric. Li finally refused. Chang threatened him and said he would get even. That was the start of the nightmares for Li Young. From that day forward, his life would change.

Li would get unsigned notes at his workstation, telling him to beware. His instincts told him he was being set up for something big—something big enough to have serious consequences. Time would reveal that his instincts were right.

The ferry ride home brought him no comfort. Li could not get the meeting off his mind. He knew heads would roll. He arrived home and greeted his mother-in-law, Jing, with a half-smile. He was polite but happy when she bid him goodbye. He wanted to be alone with his son. The sound of thunder threatened, and Jing was happy to leave. She wanted to get home before the downpour.

Li took some leftovers out of the fridge and took a pan from the cupboard. He placed the leftovers in the pan and onto the small burner to heat. He barely touched them.

~~~

The following morning called for sunny skies, with possible rain in the late afternoon. It was their day off. Li and Hua had talked about doing some shopping at the Kowloon market. They would have an afternoon where they could talk to the locals and socialize.

Li surmised Hua had heard about the missing fabric and was surprised she hadn't mentioned it to him. Was it her way of protecting him from additional stress?

"How was your night at work?" Li asked. They spoke in the Cantonese language.

"It was stressful. I suppose you heard about the missing fabric? I can't imagine who would do such a thing. I do hope they find the culprit."

"Hua, I have kept something from you. A few weeks ago, I refused to give co-workers some of my fabric. I have been threatened since." Li's throat tightened, and he couldn't speak. He paused to catch his breath. "One worker has been sending me threatening notes. I'm sure it's Chang Chao."

"Why didn't you report him?"

"Because I didn't want any trouble. You know what they would do to us. We would both be on the black list. Maybe even get fired. Besides, I know Chang Chao is the kind of person that would seek revenge."

Hua walked over to the sink and filled the kettle. She heated some noodles with egg and cut a few slices of lunch meat.

Hua placed the meal on a small wooden table, one they had picked up in a flea market before Chen was born. One side of the table was kept against the wall. It was surrounded on three sides by some old camphor wood chairs. A small blue checkered cloth covered it. There was no room for knick-knacks or a vase with a few flowers to cheer it up. They both sat in silence as they ate breakfast and sipped tea until the kettle was empty.

~~~

The brilliant Hong Kong sun beckoned Li and Hua to walk. They avoided the train, and they strolled to the pier with Chen in tow.

The Young family boarded the Star Ferry, its white steam funnel, imprinted with black stars, emitting puffs of hot vapor and its flags flapping against the wind. The ferry departed the Quarry Bay pier, passing Victoria Harbor, on its way to the Kowloon Peninsula. The wind picked up and swept across their faces as waves, topped with white foam, beat against the pilings of the pier. They watched from the upper deck as puffs of steam evaporated in the indigo sky.

When they reached the Kowloon harbor front, they walked for at least an hour. They tried to erase the pangs of doom that gnawed at them. The pangs didn't leave.

The couple walked to Salisbury Road and passed the Railway Clock Tower. Its granite and red brick facade, covered with a white dome, stood out among the other buildings. The tower had four clock faces, one on each side that indicated the time of day to passersby.

They walked the back alleys, taking turns pushing the carriage. They stepped aside from time to time to avoid the seasoned bikers who whisked through the narrow, winding paths like riders in a marathon.

Men with pointed straw hats were running from the markets, carrying bamboo poles on their shoulders. The poles held two straw baskets, one on each side, some filled to the brim with fruits while other baskets were filled with fresh-cut flowers. Some men wore flat sandals; other men were barefoot—making a living in the best way they knew how.

Li and Hua turned down a side street and passed children who were playing tag and scurrying about. They had run out from a narrow alley onto the uneven cobblestones. A little girl, Hua thought looked to be about five, fell onto the hard stones and began to cry. Hua approached her and saw her knee had a large abrasion. It was covered in redness. Hua reached into a side pocket of the carriage and pulled out her tapestry purse. She opened the purse and retrieved a small plastic bag that contained a piece of gauze she had soaked in a solution of boiled water and a pinch of salt. Next to the plastic bag was a ceramic cup, filled to the brim with aloe vera juice she had extracted from a plant growing on her windowsill. It was her own first aid kit she carried with her since Chen was born. It was a family recipe handed down from her grandparents.

Hua comforted the girl as she spoke to her in Cantonese. "What's your name?" Hua smiled.

Through her sobs, the girl answered, "Lili." Tears slid down her cheeks, blurring her vision and falling onto her white blouse, now soiled with grime. She looked about, as if she were searching for her mother. *Maybe her mother is one of the merchants,* Hua thought.

In a soft voice Hua continued to console Lili. "This might sting for a second, but it will make you feel better later, okay?"

Lili gazed into Hua's eyes, with a look of trust only a child could have. Hua cleansed her knee with the gauze and gently dabbed a small amount of the plant's gooey substance onto the wound. She covered it with a sterile bandage.

The little girl beamed, and her eyes twinkled as she gazed at Hua. "Mm goi," Lili said. The couple watched as she ran off to catch up with her friends. She maneuvered around a stand of vegetables, her silky black pigtails swaying like tiny pendulums, and she disappeared into the crowd. Li and Hua chatted about how someday Chen would be doing the same.

~~~

Li and Hua had visited the Kowloon markets often. They were among their peers, hard workers like themselves—people they loved to be around. They could feel the very pulse of the city. It was beating with eagerness and excitement. It exuberated warmth and culture and a hope for a better future. These were working people—loyal contributors. They were the backbone of their generation, the foundation and cornerstone of their society.

The Kowloon markets were plentiful, colorful, and full of energy. They were the largest Hong Kong had to offer.

Li and Hua found their way to the fresh food market. Merchants were shouting and people were rubbing elbows as they walked through the alleyways, trying to reach the next seller of whatever. Hua kept a tight grip on the carriage and did not take her eyes off Chen.

The afternoon became warmer, and Hua was tired from her last shift, she had slept but a few hours. The couple shopped for another hour. The vegetables were fresh, and Li wanted to pick up several onions, along with some squash. After making his purchase, the couple strolled to the market's live section. There were chickens and geese being sold, along with many birds in bamboo cages that hung from hooks—some exotic, some not. Hua would have loved to ask for one or two—maybe a green parrot or a canary that sang sweetly to soften her husband's troubled heart, but she dared not ask. Money was tight, and she was grateful to have enough to last until the end of the month.

The couple reached the meat and fish sections of the market. There were merchants with white aprons tied around their waist yelling out to buy their fish. There were many types of fresh and salt water species. Hua observed a merchant who was holding up a huge eel and shouting for a buyer. Her face paled and she felt weak.

The smell of fresh fish, meats, and poultry, hanging on metal hooks over the heads of the merchants, made Hua nauseous, and the words her husband revealed to her about the incident at work haunted her. She asked if they could leave. Li agreed to take her home.

On their way to the Kowloon pier, Li stopped at a stand to pick up fresh ginger. He would make Hua a pot of ginger tea when they arrived home. It would settle her stomach. He also picked out some apples and oranges. He waited as a heavyset woman, who was wearing a black bib apron, tossed them into a brown paper bag.

Li noticed Hua's skin had turned ashen, by the time they reached the pier. "I think we should stop and see the Nguyens before we board the ferry. Maybe they could give you something to ease your nausea. A ferry ride would only make matters worse."

~~~

The Nguyen families had been friends with the Young families for generations. Their ancestors were from Beijing. Bo Nguyen's marriage was arranged by her family. She married Tao Nguyen the same year the Youngs married, and it seemed to be working. They migrated to Hong Kong and moved to the Kowloon Peninsula. They settled in Kowloon West, an area known as Kowloon Tong.

Tao had a home built a few blocks west of La Salle Street, with a view of Beacon Hill, one of the highest hills surrounding Hong Kong. The northern view from their back gardens was majestic, with massive low clouds hovering over the hills so close to their peaks they nearly touched.

It had been a year since Li and Hua had seen the Nguyens. They had run into each other at a festival that was celebrated in Hong Kong city. They promised to keep in touch. With Tao's great success Li felt inferior. He thought of himself as a common laborer, one who worked in a sweatshop for minimum wages, not recognizing his own talent and creativity. Tao was a well-known attorney.

"We have a choice of how to get there," Li told Hua. "If we walk, it will take over forty minutes, and you are not strong enough. A bus can take us, and it will be cheap, but it's not the shortest route. We will walk to Jordan Road and take a taxi. It will take us to Kowloon Tong in under five minutes, depending on the traffic."

Li felt the Nguyens may be able to help Hua, with much less time it would take to board the Kowloon ferry to Quarry Bay, take the train, and walk back to their apartment.

~~~

Tao Nguyen had accumulated his wealth by opening a prestigious practice in Hong Kong. His roots traced back to a wealthy Beijing dynasty. His ancestors remained wealthy despite the past wars, and their wealth was inherited by the generations which followed.

Tao's family used their resources to send him to the United Kingdom where he attended the Dickson Poon School of Law at Kings College. He completed his post graduate studies there and returned to Hong Kong to work for a well-known law firm.

Tao felt he had learned all he had to. After several years, he opened up his own law firm, and he was known for representing the underdogs of Hong Kong. He was also known for winning ninety-nine percent of his cases.

~~~

Chen fussed a little. Hua would feed him the milk and pureed rice meal she had packed in ice and taken with her, once they arrived at the Nguyen home.

When the couple reached Jordan Road, they hailed a taxi. They stepped in the small blue Ford Anglia with the white top and sat. The taxi driver folded the carriage and placed it into the trunk compartment. Li was grateful. The driver returned to the car. "Where to?" he asked.

"Kowloon Tong." Li gave the driver the address. It took about six minutes to reach their destination.

The two-story house was majestic. Its white façade was crowned with a pagoda style black roof and a balcony that wrapped around its sides.

"Are you sure you have the right house?" Hua asked.

"I keep a list in my wallet for times like this." Li's smile was one of victory.

The driver seemed to know the area well. He pulled up to the entrance and parked the taxi. He exited the car, retrieved the carriage from its trunk and bid the Youngs goodbye. Li tipped a little extra and watched the driver as he disappeared around the corner.

Li and Hua stood in front of the Nguyens' home for a few moments before approaching the door. They surveyed their surroundings in awe. There were lush gardens circling the property with a view of the Hong Kong hills behind it.

The sky looked threatening, as dark clouds hovered overhead. Hua approached the door and knocked. At first, no one came. Her thought was she might not make it back to the ferry. She turned to her husband. "I don't think anyone is home, we'd better go."

As they turned to leave, the door swung open. Bo Nguyen stood before them. She was a petite woman. She wore a large black bun secured on the top of her head like a crown. It was held together with a beige tortoise shell comb. The comb was an heirloom handed down from several generations. It was in the shape of a fan and embellished with blue rhinestones.

Bo was wearing a two-piece outfit made of Chinese silk. Its fabric's white buds, green leaves, and brown stems, sprinkled on a background of pink silk, reminded Hua of a nature garden in springtime. Bo's eyes were large, round and dark, and her brows were thin and arched high over her eyes. She wore tan makeup and a tint of bronze blush. Her thin lips were a deep ruby color she had applied above the lip line to make her lips look plumper. She wore black silk slippers and a huge smile. Hua hardly recognized her.

"Hua," Bo yelled, "I haven't seen you and Li in ages. I'm honored, please come in."

Bo Nguyen ushered the couple into a sunroom. Hua watched Bo as she led the way. Her loose-fitting silk pants fluttered as she walked, reminding Hua of the baby sandpipers that hug the Hong Kong shoreline.

The sunroom was luxurious. Hua didn't wonder for a moment why it was called a sunroom. Its massive windows covered three sides of the area with a view of the surrounding hills; It was drenched in sunlight.

"Please sit and make yourself comfortable," Bo offered. "I'm expecting Tao at any time." Bo walked over to the carriage. "May I see the baby?"

Hua gently lifted Chen from the carriage and handed him to Bo. Her eyes became liquid as she related to Hua that she was unable to conceive. Hua realized at that moment, all the luxury in the world would not compare to being the mother of Chen Young.

"What made you make the visit to Kowloon Tong?" Bo asked, glancing at the couple.

"We were spending the day at the markets in Kowloon when Hua took sick. We were hoping you could help her. The trip home was longer than the trip to your house. Is there anything you can give her before we have to take the ferry back?" Li was concerned.

Bo walked over to Hua who was seated in a soft golden lounge chair. She felt her forehead. "No fever!" She felt her arms and her legs under her loose trousers. They were cool and damp to the touch. "Something is not right with you. I'm going to call the doctor. He lives in the apartments nearby. He is a kind man. He's semi-retired, and I'm sure he will not delay in coming."

Bo was adamant. She did not give Hua a chance to refuse the offer.

Bo left the room and returned within the minute. "The doctor is on his way," she announced.

It took only a few minutes for the doctor to appear at the door. Bo invited him in and took him straight to Hua whose complexion, by now, was paler. He bowed slightly to Li and approached Hua. He was a short man with dark brown eyes. He squinted as he introduced himself. "I'm Doctor Yong," he said.

Doctor Yong smiled at Hua. She returned the smile. She wondered if Yong was his first or last name. She didn't ask. She was uncomfortable, and she wanted to get the examination over with as quickly as possible.

The others stepped out of the room. After his examination, the doctor spoke. "Your heart seems to be in good shape, Mrs. Young, however, I think you are suffering from dehydration as well as motion sickness from the ferry ride to Kowloon. I am going to leave some medication with you. You must drink more liquids. I will check with you in the morning," the doctor offered.

Hua was weak and confused. Her dehydration had added to the dizziness and nausea she was feeling. Doctor Yong could tell she was under stress. He surmised it was personal and part of the cause. He turned to Bo. "Please see she drinks plenty of water." "Plain ginger tea is fine," he added. Bo smiled and nodded.

The doctor gave Hua an antiemetic and promised to follow up. "Have a good night's rest, and I'll see you in the morning."

"We live in Hong Kong, Doctor."

"I know, but I'm going to request you stay the night. I want to be sure you are strong enough to travel back to the island. The change of scenery may help."

Dr. Yong turned to Bo. "Is it okay with you if the Youngs stay the night?" the doctor asked.

Bo was delighted. "Of course, it would be our pleasure," she said. She thanked Dr. Yong and showed him to the door.

Li rose and ran after the doctor, offering to pay for his visit. "There will be none of that! Friends of the Nguyens are my friends also." He bowed slightly. His eyes turned to Bo. "Take good care of her. The medicine will help relieve the nausea. I will stop by in the morning to make sure she takes a second dose."

Bo had a guest room with a lovely view of the gardens. Humming a tune, she prepared the room for the Young family. She covered the bed with clean linen sheets, as white as the winter dustings that fall on the mountains of Beijing. She was almost giddy.

Tao walked in the front door around 6 p.m. He smiled and gave his wife a hug. "Will you go into the sunroom?" Bo blurted. "There's a few guests to greet you."

Li stood to greet Tao as he appeared in the doorway. Tao ran to him and gave him a hug. "Hey, old boy, it's been a while, what brings you to our little village?"

Li related what took place. Tao walked over to Hua. He took her hands in his. "Until you are better, Hua, you are most welcome to stay with us."

Bo had planned a sumptuous meal for the Youngs. It included Swedish crepes with orange butter. Hua was surprised at the menu.

"I'm trying out new things all the time," Bo said. "I suppose you are part of my culinary studies."

"You get ten stars," Hua teased.

"You haven't tasted anything yet." Bo laughed. "Are you feeling any better?" She was hoping Hua's medicine had kicked in.

"Somewhat better, thank you."

"Are you up to joining me in the kitchen while I finish preparing dinner?"

"I'd love that! I'll sit quietly and watch a master chef create a masterpiece." They both laughed.

Hua held onto Bo's arm as they walked to the kitchen. Hua's eyes turned to saucers when she saw the state-of-the-art appliances and cookware. Her own cookware consisted of two large steaming pots and several smaller pans for boiling and frying.

Hua watched with enthusiasm as Bo heated a small amount of oil in a frying pan. She tossed in a basket of mushrooms that she had chopped earlier, adding parsley and a clove of garlic. She seasoned the ingredients with thyme, salt, and pepper. After a few minutes, she added fresh spinach to the pan.

"I'm on a crepe kick," Bo said. "My entrée is spinach and mushroom crepes. For dessert, I made Swedish crepes with orange butter, stuffed with fruit and nuts and topped with sweet cream. I hope you are up to it."

Hua was amazed at the ease in which Bo cooked. She glided over the kitchen floor as if she were dancing. She wondered if Bo's two feet ever touched the floor at the same time.

Hua was still a bit queasy and Bo understood. She offered Hua some boiled chicken and broth with vegetables. Hua opted for the crepes.

After Chen was put to bed for the night, the couples sat in the sunroom and filled each other in on their lives since they had last seen each other. Bo prepared some milk tea for the men with a small pot of honey and a tray of lace cookies Tao had brought from Hong Kong. She steeped plain ginger tea for Hua.

"No…no, we've had enough tonight" "You've outdone yourself. Plain tea is fine." Li said.

"How'd I do, rating wise?" A huge smile spread across Bo's face.

"I've upgraded you to a twenty! This was the finest dinner I've ever had." Hua was sincere.

The stars were plentiful as the couples peered out into the night sky. The clouds had moved on, revealing a full moon. As Hua gazed skyward, she thought the moon resembled a giant plate of gold, resting on a cerulean cloth. She remembered the many folklore tales told to her by her grandparents that spoke of the constellations—stories of emperors and kings, of princesses and dragons, and of stars so bright they lit up the night sky like torches, and she smiled. Li caught her look. "What makes you smile so?" he asked. His grin was wide.

"It's my special secret," Hua replied. Each time she gazed toward the sky, she would smile again. Hua and Li had never experienced the heavens as they had this night.

By the end of the evening, Li confided in his friends what had taken place at the Kowloon factory. "I know Chang Chao may have had something to do with this."

Tao advised Li as best he could. "If you get accused of stealing the imported silks, please call me." He paused. "I have many commitments coming up, and I may not be available to handle your case myself, but if the time comes, I have a full staff. I will make time for your case. The staff is more than competent. Save every note this Chao guy gives you, even if they are not signed. We have ways of checking handwriting. You will not go down for something you didn't do." "Not on my watch!" he added.

~~~

The morning came too quickly for the Youngs. They had never been treated so cordially or felt so loved.

Tao offered to drive the couple to the Kowloon pier. He would park in his rented spot and take the Star Ferry back to the island with them. A friend would pick him up and drive him to his office from the pier.

Doctor Yong stopped by and gave Hua a clean bill of health. He felt she was strong enough to take the ferry home. "The walk from the train stop to home will do you good. Ask for the day off, I would like you to rest an extra day," he instructed. Li and Hua thanked the doctor.

"Take another dose of your medication tonight, and don't forget those liquids," Dr. Yong said, as he bid them goodbye.

~~~

Hua felt stronger by the minute. The bay was calm, and the sun blessed the travelers with its golden rays. It provided Hua with the warmth and comfort she needed.

Except for the larger crafts with their giant canvas sails gliding by, the images of the smaller boats on the water were no different than on the ride to the peninsula.

The larger boats were owned by people on the far side of Victoria Bay. Some were people of affluence— doctors, lawyers, and other professionals, who invested in trade and big corporations on the side. They were considered the upper crust in the Western world; many of them would have been called rich capitalists.

"When I get to the office, I will call the manager of the Kowloon factory and relay to him of Hua's illness and how you both stayed the night with Bo and me. He will excuse you and give Hua sick leave for the day," Tao offered. Not having access to a phone the couple was grateful. They shook hands and parted.

Hua wheeled the carriage to the lower deck, with Li at her side. Tao chose the upper deck. He would meet with some colleagues there.

As the wind picked up, the waters in the bay took a turn. The sky turned to slate gray, and the white clouds turned as dark as the star emblems on the steam funnel. Topped with a thick white foam, the choppy waves rolled about. Li gazed out onto the water and thought of the fancy beers offered at the pricey lager houses in Hong Kong, their steins filled with dark amber liquid and topped with a dense foam. It was a life he could never afford. Li looked down at his son who was sleeping peacefully in his carriage. The bumpy ride was not disturbing him in the least. Li thought of how rich he really was. He turned his gaze to Hua who was hovering over the carriage. He smiled. *I prefer tea to beer anyway,* he reasoned.

Hua looked out over the railing and noticed a young boy maneuvering a wooden boat about the size of a canoe. He had tacked a hand written sign on the side of the boat with the words: Water Taxi. He looked no more than fifteen. Hua imagined he was trying to make money to help his family. She opened the paper bag she had placed in a pocket of the carriage and pulled out an orange. The boy looked up at her and smiled. He took off his white cotton hat, the elements had yellowed with age, and he waved it in the cool morning breeze. The breeze blew his thick black hair around, like a silk scarf blowing in the wind. Hua threw the orange in his direction. The boy skillfully caught it in his hat. His grateful smile said thank you. He waved again and returned the hat to his head.

Hua waved back. She knew the ravages of being poor, of not knowing where your next meal would come from. If you worked, you ate. It was as simple as that!

~~~

Only time would tell if Li would be suspected of the crime at the Kowloon factory. Hua was aware the stolen fabrics would not be considered a minor incident—not with Wang Wei in charge. She also knew the highest quality material was used for the men's dress shirts, and it would be very easy for Chang Chao to devise a plan to target her husband as the culprit. She knew those who owned the factory ran it under the strictest conditions. The person responsible would most likely go to jail.

## CHAPTER FIVE
(The Investigation 1968)

The sewing machines buzzed like swarms of bees escaping from their hives. The sound continued for hours until the first mid-morning break. At the sound of the bell, hundreds of workers jumped to their feet and headed for the double doors. Some hurried to use the restrooms, others to slip outside and have a smoke.

Its echo resonating throughout the empty room, the work bell resounded, and the sewers rushed to their stations to continue sewing. There would be a short lunch break later in the afternoon with barely enough time to eat. There wasn't time to socialize and get to know your peers. Relationships did not blossom at the Kowloon factory.

A rumor was circulating throughout the factory. An investigation of every worker was being conducted, starting with the last person's station in the rear of the building. It was a one-to-one interrogation so a person could not get back up from another. Each person was called into the manager's office and questioned separately.

"Where were you on Wednesday the twelfth?" Wang Wei asked one of the sewers.

"Did you leave your station at any time, other than your breaks?" Wang asked another.

"Who did you speak to on Friday, the fourteenth?" The questions continued.

"Did you see anything odd on the weekend?"

"Do you know anyone connected to the garment black market?" Wang Wei questioned them all.

"Of course not!" Li would answer when his turn came.

The questioning went on all day, every day. It was unending. When it came time for Wang Wei to call on Chang Chao to be questioned, time stood still for Li Young.

Li eyed Chang Chao as he entered the manager's office at the back of the room. Li couldn't sew a stitch until he saw Chang open the door and return to his station.

Li sensed he would be called back. He was not. The manager, Wang Wei, had kept his word and called each one in order. Li worried several days would pass before he would be called into Wang's office. He felt he could never last that long. He said a short prayer to his god and continued trying his best not to mess up. At one point, he turned and glanced at his adversary. Chang looked up with the look of a Cheshire cat. Li caught the look and diverted his gaze. He barely managed to get through the shift.

~~~

It was another two weeks before Li was called into Manager Wang Wei's office. He eyed Li as he sat. Li gazed at the window above Wang, avoiding his eyes.

The amber sun had risen into Li's view. The sky was powder blue, and it was surrounded by puffs of cotton-like clouds. Li pictured himself in Quarry Bay Park, lying on a blanket with his wife and son, enjoying the sky's view as they ate shrimp dumplings, mixed wild rice, and mandarin orange cheese cake for dessert. His image faded.

Wang Wei's questions were the same, "Where?" "When?" "How?"

Li answered every question truthfully, but it was his demeanor that gave a different impression as he drew himself back in his chair and pressed his elbows into his sides. His body shrank before Wang's eyes. Li gazed toward the door, his heart raced, and he wanted to flee.

"Mr. Young, you have been with us for a while now, and your work has been highly respected. You have been accused of stealing twenty rolls of our best silk fabric from India. Your accuser says he can provide us with the proof. Are you able to defend yourself?"

Li couldn't speak. He asked if he could have a sip of water. Wang's hand trembled as he handed Li the cup. A small amount of water spilled onto Li's trousers, but he didn't feel a thing.

Li thankfully took the cup. He gulped half of the water down and began his defense. "It is an honor to work at the Kowloon factory. What I am saying to you, respected Sir, is the truth. I did not take your fabrics. Of course not! I would have no reason to." Li paused. "I have a wife and a young baby. I would never jeopardize my family—or my reputation."

Wang Wei continued with his accusation, although he tended to believe Li. "There is a thorough search going on at your workstation. If we find anything wrong, you will be held and convicted of the highest charges."

Li excused himself. He was polite and thanked Wang Wei for giving him the opportunity to say something in his own defense. His eyes were moist, but he was able to hold back tears from falling. He bowed slightly and turned, barely making it to the door. As he left the office, he saw several men at his station opening the drawers and checking under the sewing table. They were wearing police uniforms.

Li stood as still as a mannequin until they left. Was he to be called back to defend himself again? He hoped not.

## CHAPTER SIX
(Samuel  Mid-1990s)

Chen had prepared his first sermon. He felt his prayers were answered when he asked the Lord to give him the right message. He was unsure of how many people would come to hear him, but he promised the Lord that even if one person showed up, he would be grateful. "After all," he prayed, "if there were only one person left on earth, You would have come down and died for him." He no longer questioned it. He would make it the best sermon he could and hope someone's life would be touched by it.

~~~

There was much to do in making an old building presentable. Some of the benches had to be sanded and stained. Chen did it himself with the help of a local boy named Samuel. Chen imagined Samuel's mother, Jeanette, would say he was a good boy. He was what the world would call a bit slow, and he spent his secondary school years in a special education program. He was slow to learn, but he was eager to be taught and always ready to lend a hand. He was a loner, through no fault of his own. The kids in school were more than unkind to him, and he became used to the name calling. "Sam the sham," they would call out as he walked by them in the hallways. He felt defeated. It showed in his walk and how he hung his head on his way to his next class. At his young age he felt this was his existence—one that would never change. He accepted it. Chen became aware of Samuel's mindset, and he was determined to help change it.

One of Samuel's favorite things to do to pass the time was to go down to Camwood Lake and fish. It was his way of compensating to deal with the hurt. His mother had bought him a fishing rod a few years prior, hoping he would take up the sport. Samuel would get his tackle box and rod together and walk to the bait shop. He would usually take his dog, Archie, with him. Worms were cheap, and he used his allowance to purchase them. With his long legs and swift stride, he would make the one and one-half mile to the lake, in under seventeen minutes. On the weekends, whenever the water wasn't too choppy, he would cast his line as far out as he could and wait, eyeing the bobber diligently. On occasion, a fish would strike, and he would bring his trophy home for his mother to cook—a catfish or maybe a small bass. Those were proud moments for him.

In the summers, Samuel would volunteer to help with Vacation Bible School. He would be the 'go for' for the teachers and scurry around doing their bidding. That was until the Pastor of the church, Rev. Brian Curry, left.

The teen became depressed until Chen arrived. Samuel was elated that Chen was the new pastor and had asked him to help with projects for the church. His mother, Jeanette, noticed the change in him and set up a meeting with Chen to thank him.

Chen knew Samuel. He had met him several times when making rounds of the middle school as a junior detective for the Camwood Police Dept. He noticed Samuel looking through the chain link fence, watching the others play hand ball against the school's brick wall. Chen would see him there often.

One day Chen decided to step in. He knew the feeling of being different in a way, coming from a foreign land, and so he called out to him. "Samuel, how about throwing a few baskets on the court?" The boy was shy but willing to learn. From that day on, they became friends.

~~~

It was Friday, after the last bell sounded. Chen had decided to stop by the high school and see if he was able to catch

Samuel leaving. Chen stood by the fence and waited. Samuel appeared in the doorway and descended the brick steps. Chen spotted him and called out. Samuel smiled and walked toward the pastor. "In your free time, would you like to help me get the church up and running?" Chen asked. Samuel was more than willing. He had no words. He didn't have to speak; His wide smile revealed his answer.

~~~

After the initial task of getting rid of all the dust that had accumulated in the sanctuary, Chen asked Samuel if he would like to help restore the benches to their original shine. Samuel jumped at the chance to learn something new.

The benches were not so worn that all of them had to be sanded. There were some scuff marks and fading, which Chen considered minor problems. He decided to work on the minor problems first.

Using a combination of vinegar, water, and a small amount of liquid soap, Chen and Samuel rubbed the benches with damp cloths until the original shine appeared. They used soft cotton cloths to dry them. When the weekend was over, they had completed their project. During their breaks Chen and Samuel had many talks, and their relationship grew to one of trust.

Chen had planned to teach Samuel how to use a hand sander, but after careful thought he decided to instruct him on using the orbital sander.

There were twenty-four benches in the sanctuary space: twelve on each side. Chen was hoping in the month allotted, before his first service, there would be enough time to get the benches to look presentable. He would have to be thorough with every step of the process to avoid any injury.

Chen placed all the tools they would need across one of the church benches. "These are the tools we will need for our project," Chen said. He was slow and precise as he explained each one. "This is an orbital sander, and these are the grits which attach to it. You use a different grade as you need it, to smooth out the kinks. You will have to wear safety glasses and a mask like these," he pointed. "You don't want to breathe in any dust. After all the kinks are out, we will put on a shine with a finishing stain."

After getting permission for the project from Samuel's mother, the two were ready to start. Samuel showed up half an hour early. Chen could see Samuel was excited to begin.

CHAPTER SEVEN
(The Arrest 1968)

The Hong Kong rainy season showed no mercy to those who had to use public transportation. It started as a light shower and morphed into a torrent, as Li headed toward the Star Ferry Pier. He hadn't heard anything since the day he was called into the manager's office at the Kowloon factory. He expected he would.

Li arrived at his workstation a few minutes before six a.m. and began to set up his machine. He threaded the bobbin and opened a new roll of fabric. This fabric was gray and had a silkier feel than the one he had previously worked on. He spread his fingers over it several times and felt the smoothness of the material. It reminded him of the silky underside of an onion peel. If it were any other day, he would have smiled. He knew quality when he felt it, but he hadn't enjoyed much of anything since he was accused of stealing the blue silks.

Manager Wang Wei was watching Li Young from the glass window of his office. He walked to the window and back several times, mumbling under his breath in Cantonese. Did he sense what was about to happen would be an injustice?

A few minutes passed, and then a few more. A man dressed in an officer's uniform entered the building and knocked on the office door. Wang Wei opened the door and greeted him. "Please come in," he said. "Have a seat," Wang pointed. The officer sat. They talked for a short time.

Li was aware of what took place. His hands vibrated like the fans above his head. Wang Wei approached him, with the officer at his side. "Mr. Li Young, we have evidence you were involved in the robbery of our silk fabrics, here at the factory. This is Officer Mao. He will escort you to the Kowloon Police Station, and you can plead your case there."

Manager Wei was obviously shaken. Li was unable to speak. He felt he had said all he could in his own defense in Wang Wei's office, the day he was interrogated.

In silence, Li cleared his station. He gathered his belongings and followed Officer Mao to the police car. He was pushed into the back seat, and the officer slammed the car door. The sound exploded in Li's ears, and he felt his life had been slammed shut—forever!

## CHAPTER EIGHT
### (Prison Life 1968)

Hua's mother, Jing, was beginning to worry. Li had never been this late before. Hua had left for her late afternoon shift, and Jing was tired. She needed someone to relieve her. She was nearing eighty, and although Chen was her only grandchild, helping to raise him was taking a toll on her body. She looked forward to her walk home. She wondered why Li hadn't arrived.

Li had been arrested for the theft at the Kowloon factory. Fabric labels that matched the numbers on the stolen rolls were found at his workstation. Li knew why the tags were found and who placed them there, but he had no proof to offer of his innocence.

Li felt his insides burn, as if someone had stuck a lighted torch down his throat. He hadn't eaten since breakfast, and he was weak. He begged the officers at the station to contact his mother-in-law and explain what took place. They refused with no reason given. He knew Hua would hear what happened when she reached the factory, but he would rather have told her himself. *Jing won't leave the baby. Once Hua finds out, she will contact Jing and ask her to stay, so she can finish her shift.* They would need the money more than ever now. Unless Li was found innocent, there would be only one paycheck.

~~~

The Kowloon prison was located yards from the water's edge. It was raised high on a bluff, with a view of Victoria Harbor. Whenever they were let out for exercise, the prisoners would glance below at the fishing boats gliding by and the sampans that brushed against the pilings. They loved the sound of the horns the fancier boats made and the noisy sea gulls that swarmed around hoping to steal a bit of lunch. They would gaze out at the open water and the expanse of hills in the far distance. They looked like tiny ant hills, lined up against an azure sky. In these moments, they felt free! *Maybe one day, I will be below on the ferry to Kowloon, looking up instead of looking down,* Li thought.

~~~

Li had been incarcerated for six months and awaiting his trial. He could not afford a seasoned lawyer and turned down help from one who offered to work pro bono. He decided not to call Tao Nguyen although he offered several times. He decided he would defend himself. "I have nothing to hide!"

The accommodations at the prison were not the Hilton Hotel, but it was not a work camp either. The place was fairly clean. Li had to share a room with seven other prisoners. The room was long and narrow with a total of eight beds that were made of unvarnished green metal. Four beds were lined against each wall. At the end of one wall stood a small sink and one toilet they all had to share. There was no privacy, which greatly humbled them. Prisoner or not, the men of Hong Kong had a sense of pride.

Hua had learned to be on her own. She had no choice. She learned to pay the utility bills and the rent on time. Her mother, Jing, moved in with her and took complete charge of Chen. Hua took on extra hours, but she barely made it each month. She had hope. She was sure her husband would be exonerated of the crime he was accused of. Only time would tell.

~~~

The forecast predicted rain. The prisoners were exercising in the yard when the skies opened. The downpour came unexpectedly, but not to the cafeteria staff who had prepared the dinner menu an hour earlier. The prisoners filed in, and one by one they took their seats. The relentless rain pounded against the tiles of the roof, yet the only sound they were conscious of was the shuffling of their feet as they walked single file to their assigned tables. One more day without exercise had put them in a blue funk.

Li sat at the same table every day and talked to the same cellmates about the same things. *Life can't be worse than this!*

Beneath the prison walls, the boats docked in the harbor were tossed around like rubber toys by the angry water. Some fishermen started pulling into the bay several hours earlier. There were no coverings overhead to protect them from getting soaked in a downpour. They opted to return to the pier. Others remained out in the choppy waters to try and reach their fish quota for the day.

The prisoners couldn't catch a break. The rain was forceful, and they would remain indoors until night call. During their free time, confined to the prison walls, the prisoners scattered to different areas. Some opted to read while others played cards or chess in the game area.

Li decided to stop by the library cart and grab a book on anything he could find to help his defense. Someone had placed a large book on the bottom shelf of the cart. The book was thick with an imitation brown leather cover. It was written by a defense lawyer. The volume caught Li's eye. He plucked the book from the cart and retreated to a corner of the common area near a window. The book was written in Cantonese. The font was so small, his eyes had trouble adjusting to the traditional characters on the page. He blinked several times. He rendered his reading glasses useless.

As Li was about to return the book to the cart, he noticed a prisoner who was standing near the hallway entrance. The man was of a medium build with dark eyes and dark hair. He seemed to be smiling at Li as if he knew him. Li became uncomfortable. He briskly walked past the man and returned to the hallway that led to his cell, taking the book with him.

Several of Li's cellmates were lying on their beds, staring at the ceiling. *Why don't they make better use of their free time, read a book or write a letter,* but he never mentioned it. He remained respectful. *It's their business.* He went to his bed and continued to read until the prisoners were called back to their workstations.

Li was liked by his cell mates and often asked to throw a softball around in the yard, but he remained depressed and aloof.

~~~

As the days passed, Li forgot about the prisoner who seemed to smile at him until he would see him again out in the prison yard.

Li was watching two cellmates gambling. They were tossing dice and betting on doubles. The winner of the pot would get gum, toothpaste, soap, or a cigarette or two.

Another group was throwing a softball around. One prisoner who was watching the game glanced over at Li. He smiled and walked toward him. His name was Lok.

"Hey, why don't you get in the ballgame? I noticed you're always off on the sidelines," the stranger said.

"I'm not very good at sports, I'd rather watch." Li's eyes were focused on the ground, but he had recognized the man's smile.

"You need to get some exercise, Man, it will build you up and maybe give you an appetite. You look like you could use a meal or two."

"I'm not up for small talk." Li turned to walk away.

"Wait," Lok grabbed his arm. "I heard a bit from the grapevine if you know what I mean?"

"No, what do you mean?"

"Look, there are some men that cackle like a room full of roosters on a party line. So, you might say I was at the party."

Li was stoic. His face showed no emotion, but his adrenaline was in high gear. Lok turned to walk away. Li called out for him to stop.

"Okay, what will it cost me for this information."

"Not sure yet. I like you so maybe nothing! I have to think about it. Meet me tonight at the library cart before night call."

Li was sure Lok was messing with him. He decided not to take him up on it. "I can't, I'm busy," Li said.

"Busy with what? Are you going to a movie or something?"

"Yeah, something like that."

"Okay, suit yourself, but you will be missing out on a nice piece of hearsay."

Lok pulled out a Marlboro and lit it. He offered one to Li. He refused. "I don't smoke."

The loud speakers in the prison yard announced the dinner call, and the two men parted and walked in the opposite direction.

The cafeteria was overcrowded. The smells were the same each day; Some form of noodles or rice, served with meat and a vegetable, maybe two on holidays. Water, coffee, or tea for drink. For dessert, each prisoner was given a piece of fruit. Many foods were boiled. Through the rounded windows, you could see steam rising from the kitchen and sneaking out into the huge commissary as opaque as a sauna in a swank hotel, clouding the images of those closest to the kitchen doors.

Li disliked the noodles. He knew they were from a box or freeze dried. Hua made them fresh each day before leaving for her shift. He also disliked the sound of the trays banging and the used eating utensils being tossed into a plastic bin, like horseshoes being tossed on a stake. "It sounds like a heavy metal concert," Li would mock. His cellmates would laugh.

The prisoner's day was routine: Up at 4:30 a.m., breakfast, work, lunch, work, outdoor exercises, dinner and free time before lights out.

The library was a small area with shelves at the end of a long hall with a book cart standing next to them. Some inmates took advantage of it, most not. When night call came, all prison cells were locked down, and all activity on the prison floors ceased.

~~~

There was a laundry section on the lower floor of the prison. Because of the high temperatures, it was kept at a distance from the other work areas. It was here Li requested to work out his days until his trial. Because of his good behavior, he was assigned the position.

There were four areas, each one run by the prisoners. One area was for sorting the soiled laundry and keeping the used bed linens separate from the worn prison uniforms. The uniforms were delivered from the upper floors in bags made of heavy fabric. The draw strings on each bag were pulled tight and knotted. The bags were thrown down chutes to be collected in large rubber bins at the bottom.

Another area housed a line of massive washing machines for washing the soiled items. Further down the corridor was a drying facility. Its commercial dryers dried the clothes and linens at the highest temperatures.

A sorting room was located at the end of the hallway. Li was assigned to it. He was in charge of sorting and folding the laundered items. He wore protective gloves and a hair net, and his prison uniform had to be cleaned soon after his shift ended. As an added protection, he wore a large gray apron which wrapped around his small frame.

The familiar smell of bleach, coupled with the various scents of laundry soap and disinfectants, permeated the entire basement. The humidity created from the huge washing machines along with the heat from the commercial dryers reminded Li of the hot, muggy summers of the Hainan rainforest. He had never been to Hainan Island, but he had read enough about it.

It was here in the confines of the underbelly of the prison that Li would spend his days incarcerated.

~~~

It took another week for Lok to approach Li. This time it seemed to him that Lok was sincere in what he had to say. Li was folding bed linens when Lok walked into the laundry area. His grin was wide. "Listen buddy, I have a good tip for you and it won't cost a dime. Please hear me out. You want to get out of this place. Right?"

"Why are you being so nice to me? You really don't know me."

"Yes, that's true, but my sister does. You worked together with her at one time. That's how *I* got the job at the factory. She's a machine. She could whip out a designer dress in an hour."

"What's her name?"

"Nancy Sun-Ming. Do you remember her?"

Li had to think for a few seconds. "Ah, yes, I do. My wife and your sister took their breaks together until your sister switched to the day shift. How is she?"

"She's as tough as a general, but never mind. Listen! She heard from a group of ladies at the sweat shop; The labels they found at your workstation were planted by Chang Chao."

"I already suspected that." Li's eyes focused on the floor. Unimpressed, he continued to fold the laundry.

"That's not all," Lok said. "She and a few girls got together and decided to search Chang's workstation for evidence. Anything they could find that would help you."

Li stopped folding the linen and stared into Lok's eyes. "Are you sure?" Li's brow furrowed.

"Relax." Lok said, "It's true." Li's small eyes grew into saucers.

"Not only am I *sure* there is evidence, the girls found a roll of designer labels and swatches of the blue silk fabric hidden at Chang's workstation. Chang's stock was white cotton. He had no business having them. They also found out that Chang is connected with the garment black market. That would be tough to prove, but leave it to them they are warriors." Lok continued, "I bet Chang got a pretty penny for the fabrics."

Li gasped. His eyes filled with tears. "What shall I do next?" he asked.

"My sister Nancy likes your wife. She misses the time they spent together. She wants to help. She's willing with the help of her two friends to take photos of the labels and the swatches they found at Chang's workstation. She's also willing to talk with the manager who accused you, Mr. Wang Wei."

Li dropped to the floor. He wrapped his arms around Lok's legs. He almost kissed his feet. He wanted to. Lok was touched. "Get up, no need for that. It will be fun to see Chang squirm. I never liked him anyway."

## CHAPTER NINE
### (Samuel's Achievement - Mid-1990s)

If anyone has ever been to Camwood, they would know it's a quaint, small part of Americana with a population of around 25 thousand people—give or take a few. Its streams intertwine gracefully into the rivers, and the rivers intertwine into the lakes, like the braids of an innocent child. The boutiques and cafes which surround the town square, the cultural arts center, and the all seasons activities offered to its visitors draw tourists from all over the world. The local merchants are friendly people with home grown businesses, handed down from the generations before them. There are artisans who create pottery, leather, and colored glass. There are chocolatiers, bakers, brewers, and candle makers. Even a farrier can be found to the delight of some local grass roots farmers who still use horses to help plow.

Although spring, summer, and fall are the busiest seasons, the winters always welcome those who toboggan and ski. After a run on the nearby mountain slopes, a trip to the sauna is not unusual. Young students on winter break gather in these cozy resorts and sit around large stone fireplaces, drinking and hoping to hook up with someone of the opposite sex.

Ice skating on the frozen lakes, which are monitored for safety, is a must, and sitting around a fire pit at night, having a song fest, toasting marshmallows, and sipping hot cider are favorite activities for the under twenty-five crowd.

Having migrated from Hong Kong when he was a teenager, Chen had grown to love his country and this town which he considered his home. He hoped one day to be able to send for his parents.

~~~

Chen and Samuel had worked for days sanding the church benches that needed repair. This day was cooler than usual. Chen decided he would teach Samuel how to use the finishing stain. "It will bring each bench that needs it back to its original shine," Chen explained. The drying time would be faster with the colder temperature. He opened all the doors and cranked open the bottoms of the stained glass windows.

A breeze swept through the sanctuary. Chen glanced over at the teenager and noticed he was smiling. Samuel knew he was about to embark on a new assignment.

Samuel had done well with the orbital sander. Chen had overseen each step, teaching him how to make long, smooth strokes in the direction of the grain and praised Samuel for it. Chen was careful to instruct him on all the safety hazards. He had guided Samuel's hands until he felt he could be on his own. Now that the task was completed, Chen would teach Samuel how to put the finishing stain onto the church benches.

The glow that was missing on the first day of Chen's arrival permeated the sanctuary. The colors of amber, magenta, blue, and emerald pierced through the stained glass windows, the sun's rays capturing their essence. Chen looked about the room. He breathed a sign of contentment. It's a work of art, he thought. This was home. This is what he wanted. It was God ordained.

## CHAPTER TEN
### (Kowloon 1968 -The Evidence)

Lok's sister, Nancy, arrived at the Kowloon factory an hour early. She walked to her workstation. This was the morning her two friends agreed to meet with her and help her find evidence to clear Li Young of the charge of robbery. They had met the night before and decided that one girl would divert Chang Chao should he arrive earlier than usual. Her friend would keep watch in the outer room near the entrance doors. The other girl would stay behind with Nancy. She would go through Chang's workstation opening drawers and boxes of textiles every worker kept stored. Nancy would take photos of the hidden designer labels and the swatches of blue silk they had seen weeks earlier. Had Chang kept the stolen swatches at work to show prospective buyers connected to the black market? She wondered.

Nancy had contacted her brother, Lok, earlier in the week. He was serving a short stint in jail for passing bad checks. She told him what they had witnessed.

"Why didn't you take photos?" Lok asked.

"We didn't have time, we would have been caught," Nancy responded.

This day was different. The girls had a mission and they were determined to complete it. Nancy took her position in front of Chang's workstation. She checked the clock on the wall and synchronized it to the hand wound Timex on her right wrist. "Check the drawers and boxes, and see if there are any pieces of evidence we could use," Nancy instructed her friend.

Nancy began snapping photographs of the entire area. She motioned to her accomplice to lift the sewing machine.

"Hurry," she said, "the work bell is about to sound." The blue swatches and the labels were right where Chang had placed them.

Nancy's friend in the outer room signaled her; the workers were arriving to begin their shift.

As quickly as they had investigated the area, the girls returned everything to its proper place, making sure nothing was amiss. As they turned to leave, Nancy's elbow knocked against a small box that had been placed on Chang's sewing table. It caused the metal container to drop to the floor. The lid popped off and landed a foot away. Hundreds of shiny buttons dropped out of the box and covered the planked flooring that surrounded Chang's work area.

Nancy froze. Her friend saw the look. Immediately she took action. She grabbed a small whisk broom that was leaning against the window on a side wall. It was attached to a hand shovel. She scooped the buttons up and placed them in the box. The girls hurried to their stations as Chang came walking through the doors.

Nancy couldn't remember if her friend had covered the box with its metal lid. Her friend was not in eye range so she couldn't signal to her. Chang took his seat and began to sew. She hoped the lid would go unnoticed.

## CHAPTER ELEVEN
(The Kwans 1968)


The 1920s had brought social and political changes to the United States. The economy grew, as most young people moved to the inner cities. It was known as a consumer society and became a society of affluence. The era was known as the roaring twenties.

As some Americans were enjoying this change of culture, factories began to evolve in Hong Kong and on the Kowloon Peninsula. One of them, established in the early 1930s, was owned by the Kwan family. It was passed down to the generations that followed, and the Kwan name became familiar and respected in the community.

At first, the factory produced china and ceramics, but the competition became too challenging for them. The Kwan family decided to explore another avenue. Fashion.

~~~

The typhoon of 1960 had reared its ugly head; its name was Mary. After the rebuilding of Hong Kong, textile and clothing factories sprung up. Fashion took root and the Kwans decided to give it a try. They took the reins and launched one of the first clothing factories on the peninsula. They knew the ins and outs of running a company, hiring many employees, and keeping ledgers. It was a good move, and it paid off. Their production of clothing became a great success.

Nothing had been modernized at the Kwan factory. The original flooring remained. Their planks were made of wide refurbished brown pine boards of different lengths. It was not unusual to hear creaking sounds when hundreds of workers walked over them during a typical work day. The work bell rang out precisely at 6 a.m. every morning. The factory functioned seven days a week with employees each getting one day off. Some factories had more than two shifts, which cut the working time down and gave employment to others, but not the Kwan factory. The shifts were long and gruesome.

~~~

The morning bell sounded, and the sewers piled in and rushed to their stations. Nancy watched as Chang Chao sewed. She was satisfied he had found nothing amiss. She was sure everything was put back as she had found it. She was able to relax.

When the second bell rang out for morning break, the room emptied in under a minute, as if someone had pulled the fire alarm. Nancy's friends had left the room, but she remained. She was riveted to her seat. She groped around and appeared to be rearranging her materials.

Chang noticed Nancy hadn't gone on break. He grinned. He had had a crush on her when they were in grade school. After years of her shunning him, he gave up, but he would still flirt with her from time to time.

Chang rose from his seat and strolled in the direction of Nancy's workstation. His lips curved upward, revealing his yellow teeth. Nancy ignored him. He continued to walk toward her; the girl that wanted him arrested; the girl that wanted him prosecuted for being a thief and for destroying the life of a good man.

Chang's sly grin morphed into a wide smile. Nancy looked at him and returned the gesture with a half-smile.

Without warning, the old pine board beneath Chang began to crackle, as if he were walking on delicate eggshells. The sound resonated throughout the room, causing Chang to look at his feet. There were crushed iridescent buttons everywhere as his work shoes forced them against the aged wooden flooring. The sound reminded Nancy of the broken tortoise shells when they are tossed by the wind at Turtle

Cove Beach. Witnessing the mishap, Nancy went into a full-blown panic.

"What's this?" Chang's tone was clueless.

"What's what?" Nancy stood and turned toward Chang.

"Buttons. I stepped on white buttons. A hundred of them."

Nancy swallowed hard. Her thoughts raced to the metal lid. "Maybe the lid on the button box was loose." She paused, waiting for Chang to respond. He didn't. "Have you dropped it recently?"

Chang turned away; his were hands clenched. Shaking his head he returned to his sewing station. He lifted the box and examined it. "No, it's on tight, right where I left it." "Maybe it's someone else's. Some of us use the same buttons, you know."

Nancy relaxed. "I have to meet the girls outside, I have no time to chat. See you around," she said politely and walked out of the room.

~~~

The day of his trial was growing near, and Li wanted to keep his mind occupied, so he asked for extra laundry duty. He hadn't talked to Lok since he had approached Li in the laundry area, and he was unsure if Lok was telling him the truth. So, he avoided him.

Lok was busy in one of the prison workshops, making traffic signs. It was his visitation day, and Nancy had arrived early. She was directed to the visiting area and waited.

Lok entered the room and smiled at his sister. Nancy spoke above a whisper as she told him of the photos she had taken. He encouraged her to speak to Manager Wang Wei before the trial and to contact Li's lawyers so that he would have a chance to make his defense.

~~~

Nancy arrived fifteen minutes before the rest of the sewers. She went to Wang Wei's office and knocked softly on the door.

"Enter," the manager said. "Make it fast, we have little time."

Nancy walked into the room and stood before him. "Manager Wei, I respectfully ask that you would listen to what I have to say." Nancy's friends waited outside. Their ears were pressed against the door, hoping to hear every word.

"What do you have to tell me, Miss Nancy?" he asked, offering her a chair. "Please sit."

Nancy was trembling. She sat and tried to hide her hands in her lap. Her throat had tightened to the point she could no longer speak. Noticing, the manager handed her a paper cup filled with iced water and sat at his desk. He pointed his index finger at her. "Continue, please."

"Mr. Wei, I think you have accused the wrong person of stealing your expensive blue fabrics," she blurted. She took a sip of the cold liquid.

"What makes you think that?" Wang asked. His voice wavered as he leaned in.

"My friends and I have been watching the man who accused Li Young of stealing the fabrics. He and his co-workers have been acting strange ever since Li Young was taken to jail. We saw Chang Chao with the blue swatches that day. We watched as he put them in the space under his sewing machine," Nancy lied. "We took the liberty to take photos of the swatches. We also took pictures of the designer labels that were delivered with the blue silk fabrics."

Nancy placed the images before Wang Wei. "These are the photos, they are all here."

Wang Wei fell backward in his chair. His warm skin turned pale. He was horrified and humiliated. To think his most respected worker was sent to jail because of his testimony. He could not look at Nancy; He gripped the sides of his head and covered his ears. He remained silent for about a minute. "Miss Nancy, are you absolutely sure of this?"

"You see the photographs, they are right in front of you," she said, pushing them closer. "Pictures don't lie!"

Wang Wei recognized that the workstation was indeed Chang Chao's. "Miss Nancy, I thank you. I will waste no time in trying to set this tragic happening straight."

Nancy left the room and returned to her workstation. She gazed at Chang Chao as he sewed. He was smiling— smirking really. Her thoughts went to Li Young who had spent six months of his life away from his wife and baby in the Kowloon jail. *Maybe by tomorrow that smile will be wiped off your face.*

## CHAPTER TWELVE
### (Chen's First Sermon - Mid-1990s)

The Living Word Church had been open for several days. Chen kept the sanctuary available twenty-four hours, in case someone should stop in for private prayer and meditation. He was about to put the finishing touches on his sermon. He entered his study with the hope that his message to the congregation would touch those who came to hear it. He walked across the room and sat in the green leather wing chair that had been donated by one of the Camwood residents. He was short in stature, and the chair enveloped him as if its wings were the arms of God, protecting him from harm. He prayed many great sermons would be written from this chair, but this night he would concentrate on a simple message.

Chen's study had floor to ceiling oak bookcases that lined the west wall. They were filled with books of various titles, most books having a Christian message. Many had been donated, some were bought. Chen had set a goal to read as many as he could and hoped to get inspiration from them.

The subject of his first sermon would be God's mercy. He reasoned there are all kinds of sin in the world, but no matter how severe the offenses, with true repentance, God, through His Son's sacrifice, will forgive them all. He made it a point to stress there is no forgiveness without repentance, and with true repentance usually comes tears. He used Peter as an example. After denying Christ three times, as Jesus had predicted, tradition tells us Peter's remorse was so deep that the tears he shed left crevices in his cheeks.

Chen knew the deep pangs of remorse. For a time, he had lived a life of crime. But he also knew of God's forgiveness. "You need only to accept His Son's sacrifice for sin at Calvary. Repent and believe, it's that simple," Niki had told him when she introduced him to her God.

Chen spent the remainder of the night going through the gospels and pinpointing the times when Jesus confronted sinners. Did He accuse? Did He point the finger? No, He always approached them in love, showing them a way out of their lifestyle. In many instances it resulted in healing of both body and soul, and many went on to do great things for God.

Chen remembered one occasion when Christ *did* show anger. It was the first day of Passover week. Many had traveled to Jerusalem to attend the feast. When Jesus entered the outer court of the temple He observed merchants selling cattle, sheep, and doves. Some were to be used for temple sacrifices. They must have been making a racket, all of them shouting out at the same time in order to make a sale. Jesus knew they were not only desecrating the temple, but they were tipping the scales to gain a profit by cheating. He could see into their very souls.

The area of worship was beyond the court. Those who came to pray were distracted by the outcries. This is why He called the temple court "a robbers' den," telling the merchants they were turning His Father's house into a market place.

There are times when anger is justified. It's called righteous anger. When someone is encouraging you to do anything that would go against your morals or your religious convictions, whether it be a certain group of people or even a government, we as Christians should stand up for what is right. Speak the truth to them; pray for them. Chen would end his sermon with these words.

It was after midnight when Chen closed the lights and settled in for the night.

## CHAPTER THIRTEEN
### (Hong Kong 1968 - The Trial)

It was Thursday, the third of October. The trial would commence at 9 a.m. The day was overcast. Gray and white clouds, moving quickly in the dense sky, were about to erupt. The Quarry Bay fishermen had taken their boats out early, unsure of how the fish would react to the changing current. They had anticipated a storm in the afternoon.They could hear thunder rumbling in the distance but not yet clashing. Sampans bobbed up and down as they brushed against the pilings of the pier.

Captains of the larger boats returned to the pier early. One by one they lowered their canvas sails as they navigated into the harbor, the men bringing in a half-day's wages.

~~~

The trial would be held in District Court. It was located west of Harbor Road in Hong Kong. It was a modern building which rose several stories. On a clear day, those fortunate enough to have their offices located on the south side of the building enjoyed the view of Victoria Harbor and the Kowloon Peninsula.

The Kwon family, who owned the Kowloon factory, was respected by most people who lived on the island. When they lost their plea for the trial to be held in Low Court, they were furious. The amount they lost from the robbery would not exceed the amount of money it would take to send the trial to a higher court, so their plea was denied. They retaliated by demanding a jury trial.

Many trials in District Court were held with one judge who reached a verdict without the help of a jury. Because of the Kwon family's influence in the community and in order to keep the peace, the court gave in to their demands. A jury trial was ordered.

~~~

The lawyers were going over their notes and opening and closing arguments when their witness arrived. Nancy Sun-Ming was ready to go on the stand, and she was warned to tell the truth and nothing but! The prosecuting attorneys were prepared to question her.

Nancy had lied, and she admitted it. She had seen the blue swatches and the designer labels in Chang's possession when he showed his co-workers, but she did not see him place them in the space beneath the sewing machine. Anyone could have placed them there, and the Kwon lawyers knew this. The argument could be Chang had discovered them himself. After all, there were two shifts.

The real question was where were the stolen fabrics? Were they still in Chang Chao's possession, or had he sold them in the black market? Nancy was warned, if there were any inconsistencies in her testimony the case would implode.

Her lawyers had made it clear to Nancy that before she gave her testimony she would have to explain to Manager Wang Wei that she did not see Chang Chao put the swatches and labels in the space beneath his sewing machine. She would also have to admit that she and her friend had invaded his work space without permission. In other words, they snooped! Wang Wei was well aware of this; he had seen the photographs. If he objected, he would have said so. But the lawyers were not convinced. Shen and Ping had given Nancy 48 hours to make things right. Today was the day she would stand up in court, and her statements would go on the court records.

The Wu brothers had volunteered to take Li's case. They had heard Li was going to speak in his own defense.

They stepped in, pro bono. Both lawyers had known the Young family. Shen Wu had gone to school with Li's cousin who he respected. When he heard of Li's plight, Shen was honored to do it. His brother, Ping, agreed.

Li was grateful, in a way. He was beginning to think he needed professional counseling, and he hesitated to contact Tao Nguyen's office, as Tao had offered the night they stayed at his home in Kowloon Tong.

~~~

Nancy Sun-Ming had arrived at the courthouse with her two friends in tow. They sat in the first row on the right side of the room, next to the defense attorneys.

The Wu lawyers would await their turn to question their witness. They decided they would call only Nancy to the stand. This would leave little room for contradiction.

All three girls were dressed in Western clothing which did not please the lawyers. Their outfits were short, above the knee, and tight. Two girls wore large flowered prints, which would cause a distraction in any assembly.

Nancy's hot pink dress was a solid color, nevertheless, she would turn any man's head.

The brothers approached the girls and asked if they would go home to change their clothing. "How can you breathe in those dresses?" Ping asked.

The girls laughed. "We try to keep up with the fashions we make," Nancy replied.

"It's not going to help the case, Miss Nancy." Ping checked his watch. It was too late, the Kwan family had entered the courtroom with the prosecution team close behind. They took their seats on the opposite side of the first row with an aisle separating them from the defense team.

The court officer stood facing the spectators. "All rise," he shouted, "this Court is now in session." Silence followed.

The Honorable Ren Chow walked out of his chamber and onto the bench. Keeping with the tradition of Great

Britain, he was donned in a long black robe and wore a wig of lacey white wool that reached beyond his shoulders; to him it was a sign of distinction. His shirt was white and ruffled. He lifted his head and smiled. The lingering chatter subsided as late spectators continued to fill up the seats.

Outsiders came; people who had heard reports on the radio or television. Strangers from all classes of society: doctors, lawyers, teachers, merchants, and blue-collar workers—they all came. The gossip had spread across Hong Kong like wildfire, and Li Young became its victim.

There was a commotion coming from the hall outside the doors. A group of teenagers had skipped school and decided to try and gain entrance into the courtroom. Maybe they were relatives of Chang Chao's or friends of his younger brother, Feng, or maybe they were just curious teens who wanted to witness a trial. One teen pulled on the brass handles of the double doors and stuck his head into the courtroom. "Close those doors!" Ren Chow barked.

The court officer ran to the double doors and shut them. Ren Chow mumbled under his breath, questioning how the teens were able to get past the guards. "Hao beishang," he hissed.

In the back of the room, reporters scurried to find a seat, notebooks in hand, each one hoping to get the scoop of the day.

One well-known reporter, Sky Wong, wrote for the Tin Tin Daily. He had his own byline, and his columns usually made the early edition. Today's column would be a shoo-in to beat it to the presses.

Li Young, who had arrived a few minutes earlier, sat to the left of the Wu brothers. He seemed a bit weak and he kept his head down as if he were already declared guilty. Judge Ren Chow called for order in the Court, and the trial commenced.

The Plaintiffs, who were members of the Kwon family, were present as well as the manager of the Kowloon factory, Mr. Wang Wei. Mr. and Mrs. Kwon, along with their daughter and two sons, sat to the right of their legal team. The aisle between them and the Defendant and his team kept them from rubbing elbows. Li could sense their icy stares.

Both team representatives were prepared to give their opening statements. The Kowloon lawyer, who represented the prosecution, was so sure of himself, he was hoping the case would be wrapped up in two days.

The prosecuting attorney described how the evidence was found at Li Young's workstation and smugly insinuated the case was a slam dunk. Chang Chao was set up, he pled.

Ping Wu stepped up to plead for the defense and presented his opening statement. He described how Li Young was a simple man who had worked hard at his job. He stressed his client would have no reason to steal anything from the factory he worked so hard for, and Li Young had earned an impeccable reputation at his craft. He was a young father with an infant at home, and he would not jeopardize his income for twenty rolls of designer fabric.

Ping Wu paced back and forth, waving his arms and looking directly into the eyes of each juror as he finished his statement: "Ladies and Gentlemen of the jury, tell me why a man with the reputation of Li Young would take a chance of losing his job and his family to spend many years in a prison cell? He is an honored and respected man. Would he jeopardize his honor also? It's ludicrous to even surmise such a thing. He has no ties with the garment market, black or otherwise! It is clear Mr. Li Young was set up by someone in his department. We have proof as well as witnesses who can attest to the crime being committed by Mr. Chang Chao at the Kowloon factory. Please take into consideration all the evidence that will be presented in this case and render a verdict of not guilty."

You could hear the gasps as Ping went on for another few minutes and closed by thanking the jury for their time.

Chang Chao had been brought in and was sitting next to the prosecuting attorneys. He was short and round. His face was wide, and his yellow teeth revealed the marks of a chain smoker. His co-workers had ditched him. They wanted nothing to do with a court case. Chang was on his own, and they told him so. There was no one to defend his character.

The prosecution team listened to Ping Wu. They showed no reaction. They had accused Li Young of the same crime, stating it was he who set up Chang Chao. The battle was about to begin. Both sides had presented their statements, and Judge Ren Chow ordered a recess for one hour.

~~~

The hour was over, and everyone took their seats. Li's lawyers had a hard time deciding which defense to bring up first. Should they show the evidence they believed they had, or should they call their witness to the stand? They decided the photographs could wait. They would call their witness, Miss Nancy Sun-Ming.

Nancy had kept her promise to the lawyers. She confessed to Manager Wang Wei that she had seen Chang with the blue swatches and the labels, but she did not see him place them in the hidden space beneath the sewing machine. Wang understood her desire to help Li Young. In fact, he was glad. He agreed to have Nancy rewrite her statement at the Kowloon factory.

Ping Wu called Nancy Sun-Ming to the stand. Nancy strolled, turned, and she faced the Court. Her hot pink dress spoke for her. There were gasps and mumblings as the court officer approached her. "Please raise your right hand." She raised her hand and repeated the words: "I do solemnly, sincerely and truly declare and affirm that the evidence I shall give shall be the truth, the whole truth, and nothing but the truth." Nancy sat, and Ping Wu began the questioning.

"Miss Sun-Ming, will you please state your full name before this Court and spell it," Ping Wu requested.

"My name is Nancy Sun-Ming, N-A-N-C-Y, S-U-N-M-I-N-G."

"How old are you, Miss Sun-Ming?"

"I'm 23 years old."

"Can you tell this Court where you live?"

"I live on the Kowloon Peninsula."

"How long have you lived on the Kowloon Peninsula?"

"All my life."

"And where do you work, Miss Sun-Ming?"

"I work at the Kowloon factory."

"How long have you worked at the Kowloon factory?"

"A little longer than three years."

"Do you know the Defendant, Mr. Li Young?"

"Yes."

"How long do you know the Defendant?"

"I've known him for as long as he has worked at the Kowloon factory."

"How long is that, Miss Sun-Ming?"

"You're his lawyer and you don't know how long he's been there?" Nancy shifted her position, and the courtroom erupted in laughter.

"Is he in the courtroom today?" Ping asked, his face a bit ruddy.

"Yes."

"Can you point him out to this Court?"

"He's over there." Nancy pointed.

"Can you tell this Court how close in proximity your workstation is to Mr. Li Young's station?"

"His workstation is about three rows in front of mine." She gestured with her hands.

"Do you have a clear view of his station?"

"Yes, a very clear view."

"Can you tell me if you have a clear view of Mr. Chang Chao's workstation?"

"He sits about two rows diagonally behind me. To see him I have to turn my head to the right. Yes, I have a clear view."

"Thank you Miss Sun-Ming, you answered my next question of what position you would take to view his station. Why are you here today, Miss Sun-Ming?"

"I am here to bear witness to the innocence of Mr. Li Young a respected co-worker at the Kowloon factory."

"Do you have any proof to back up what you are saying, Miss Sun-Ming?" Ping Wu asked.

"Yes, I do."

"Why don't you tell this Court what you mean by that, and please be specific, what you say will go onto the court records."

Nancy appeared rattled. She shifted her position several times until she felt comfortable. With each shift of her body, her tight dress wrinkled. She used her palms and pressed hard, trying to iron the wrinkles out, like the steam pressers iron the shirts at the Kowloon factory. She went on with her testimony.

"Respected Sir, on this particular day I had arrived to work at the Kowloon factory earlier than usual. No one else had arrived except Chang Chao and two of his co-workers. They were standing in front of Chang's workstation and whispering. Chang opened a small box and showed his friends its contents. His friends gasped, and one friend immediately closed the box. Chang laughed and opened it again. I heard him say in a whisper, 'What are you worried about, it's all good.'"

Nancy continued. "He took out labels a designer had sent to the factory and blue swatches of an expensive grade of material."

"How did you know the material was an expensive grade?" Ping asked.

"It was lightweight and shiny," Nancy replied. "It looked like an expensive silk." She paused. "I do know my materials, you know!" Again, courtroom laughter followed.

"Continue please," Ping said, unembarrassed.

"I had never seen this material before. I was watching from my workstation. It was at that point Chang's friend noticed me. I looked away and started to arrange my quota for the day. I felt something was amiss from the beginning. Later that day, I saw Li Young sewing a man's dress shirt using the same material. It was not the usual cotton fabric we are used to working with in our department. This was of a greater quality. I knew Li had been chosen to work with it. He was capable. Chang wasn't." Nancy sighed and looked directly at Judge Ren Chow.

"Go on," Ping said.

"Chang and his friends often badgered Li for extra fabric, because they made so many sewing errors. Li may have refused…"

"Objection," the Prosecuting Attorney shouted. "She's speculating. The witness is insinuating my client may have set Li Young up for revenge."

"Objection sustained," the Judge said. He addressed the court stenographer. "Will the Court please strike 'Li may have refused,' from the record. Miss Sun-Ming can you please rephrase your statement?"

"Sorry, Your Honor." Nancy continued, "I saw Chang Chao approach Li Young a number of times for his fabrics, because Chang made so many errors he ran out of his quota for the day." Nancy swallowed hard and cleared her throat. "As far as the blue silks are concerned Chang had no reason to use them. His assignment was working with white cotton of a cheaper grade. Why was he holding the samples?"

"Leave the questioning to the lawyers, Miss Sun-

Ming," Judge Ren Chow ordered. He looked at Ping Wu. "Continue."

Pressing her palms against her thighs, Nancy continued to iron her dress.

Before the Kwon lawyer could object to her question Ping Wu stopped Nancy from speaking further. He requested to approach the bench. "Your Honor, I request a recess at this time. I can see the witness is having difficulty speaking." Ping Wu looked at his brother and waited.

"Permission granted. One hour," Judge Ren Chow said. "Miss Sun-Ming, you may step down."

~~~

During recess, both Wu lawyers took Li Young aside in an outer room, and Nancy disappeared into the rest room. The outer room was empty. Ping Wu spoke first. He reiterated what he had asked a hundred times. "Li, did you at any time give the designer material to Chang Chao or any one of his friends."

"No Sir, I did not...I would never..." *I'm shocked and disappointed they would think that.* But Li understood there would be questions they would have to ask on the stand.

The Wu Lawyers trusted Li Young completely. They asked no further questions, and all three men returned to the courtroom.

~~~

Nancy Sun-Ming returned and stood before the Court. She was asked to swear in again. Judge Ren Chow instructed her to continue with her testimony. Her hands vibrated like the motor on one of the boats in the harbor. Her throat tightened, and she thought she would be unable to continue. The court officer offered her a cup of cold water. "Thank you," she said gratefully. "Your Honor, I must apologize for what I am about to reveal to this Court." She paused. "I am truly sorry." Nancy felt her cheeks burn. "Along with two of my co-workers, we decided to investigate on our own, in order to help my friend and co-worker, Mr. Li Young. We planned a time and day that we would meet at the Kowloon factory. We would go over Chang's workstation looking for any clues that would help our friend. One co-worker would wait outside, and I would approach Chang's station with another. I had seen Chang with the blue swatches and the labels before. It was a matter of finding them. On this particular morning, before anyone else had entered the factory, my co-worker and I searched Chang's station. At one point we decided to lift the sewing machine to look into the deep space beneath it. We found the box containing the blue swatches and the designer labels there." "The photos we took will prove it," she added.

The Kwon family lawyer jumped from his seat. "I object, Judge, I demand that be struck from the record. Someone could have placed the swatches there." The court officer walked over to both Kwon lawyers and whispered to them; they were to refer to the Judge as Your Honor from now on. The Judge scowled.

"True, Your Honor," Nancy replied, "but my womanly instinct told me it was Chang who placed the swatches and labels there." Nancy straightened herself in the chair. She crossed her arms and legs, and she smirked. Once more the courtroom erupted in laughter, and the Wu Lawyers cringed.

Chang Chao's jaw stiffened, and his face was as red as the summer gooseberries brought in from the mainland.

"Objection sustained." It was clear the Judge was frustrated.

"May I remind the prosecuting team that Miss Sun-Ming is describing what she says she witnessed. She has testified that she and her friend saw the fabric swatches and labels in the space under the sewing machine. This is what she claims. This is why she is here. You are accusing Li Young of the same crime." The Judge gazed at Nancy.

"However, Miss Sun-Ming, will you please refrain from adding your opinion of who is guilty."

Judge Ren Chow rolled his shoulders and pointed to the court stenographer. "Strike Miss Sun-Ming's last statement from the record," he instructed.

"May I say one thing before you call me off the stand, Your Honor?"

"Go ahead, Miss Sun-Ming, if you think it will help the case."

"I know you think I've made up my mind that my co-worker, Li Young, was set up…"

"Objection," the lawyer for the prosecution shouted.

"Objection overruled. I want to see where Miss Sun-Ming is going with this." The Judge looked at Nancy. "Continue with your statement."

"Your Honor, I failed to say that the labels in question are not sewn onto the garment by the sewer of the shirts. The labels are sewn by an inspector after a thorough inspection of the garment is completed. That's done in the Labels Room. The sewer is never given the labels at any time." "There is no need for Mr. Li Young or Chang Chao to have had them," she added.

There was a gasp heard throughout the courtroom. Nancy continued with her testimony. "However, if a label was found at Mr. Li Young's station, I would be less suspicious than if a label was found in Chang Chao's possession. These were specific labels for that fabric only and meant for the designer's shirts. They are sewn on by the inspectors of the product, not by the sewer of the shirts. This is done in a separate area of the factory."

"Objection…she's speculating again." The Kwon lawyer shouted.

"Objection overruled." "This is vital information that was not brought to light before. You will have your chance to cross examine the witness." The Judge tightened his lips, but the Wu brothers detected a slight smile as they were motioned to the bench.

"Gentlemen, do you plan on calling Miss Sun-Ming's co-workers to the stand at any time to corroborate her testimony?" Judge Ren Chow asked.

"Yes, Your Honor, if necessary." Shen Wu replied.

Several more outcries erupted from the prosecution side before Nancy finished her testimony. Judge Ren Chow demanded order in the court, banging the gavel several times against its sound block.

"Miss Sun-Ming, you may step down from the stand," the Judge instructed.

Nancy Sun-Ming had managed to plant a seed of doubt in the minds of an entire courtroom. The Judge remained silent for a moment, however, his smile revealed his thoughts. *Well done!* As he rose from his seat, he slammed the gavel against its sound block for the last time. "Court adjourned until tomorrow, 9:00 a.m."

## CHAPTER FOURTEEN
### (Hong Kong 1968 - Two Witnesses)

Shen and Ping Wu had been up half the night trying to piece together their defense. How were they to make the photographs seem convincing to the jury? Judge Ren Chow agreed, anyone could have placed the evidence in the deep space under Chang Chao's sewing machine. They would no longer be able to use the swatches and labels as convincing evidence.

"We have to come up with something that will implicate Chang Chao. Finding the boxes that contain the rolls of missing silk fabrics is our only real defense." Shen Wu said.

"If they were sold on the black market, the silks no longer exist," Ping responded. "There must be someone who knows what really happened. Someone who would be willing to testify against Chang Chao."

Because the defense team was accusing Chang Chao of setting up the defendant, Li Young, Chang was on leave from work, pending the outcome of the trial. He would not be able to move the silk fabrics if they were still at the Kowloon factory. The Wu lawyers knew it was a long shot; if they had not been sold on the black market, the silks had to be where Chang had hidden them.

"What if we speak to the two workers who refused to testify in Chang's behalf? Ping questioned. What if we told them they would be questioned sooner than later. If they cooperated with us, it could be our hidden advantage."

"We don't know if they ever saw the fabrics," Shen answered. They only saw the swatches and labels."

"You don't know that, it's worth a try."

It was after midnight. With a few calls and the help of several workers at the Kowloon factory Shen and Ping Wu were able to track down Chang's two co-workers. They agreed to meet in a Hong Kong bar, located near pier 7, Quarry Bay, at one a.m.

~~~

The bar was as dense as the fog outside. Rock music was blasting from the loudspeakers as the two lawyers entered through the double glass doors. The room was filled with smoke, and the lighting was poor; The lawyers took several minutes to find their prospective witnesses.

The two men were seated near a side window, waiting for the lawyers to arrive. One sat close to the window. The other man sat on the opposite side of a round teakwood table. They were tapping their fingers to the music on the table's wooden surface until the lawyers appeared. Shen and Ping Wu approached them and extended their hands.

It was not unusual for families in Hong Kong to give their children Western first names; The lawyers were not surprised when the men introduced themselves.

"I'm Jimmy Lau, and this is my co-worker Jackie Yuan," Jimmy said. He cleared his throat, and the men shook hands.

Jimmy was short in stature with cropped, straight hair. His black hair shined as the light above casted its glow onto the table. Jackie was taller and robust. His hair was long and pulled back in a tight pony tail. He wore tortoise shell glasses, and his constant blinking told Shen Wu that the man needed a new pair. Both men were dressed in jeans and T-shirts, their jean jackets hanging over the edge of the black vinyl booths.

Shen Wu spoke first. "Gentlemen you know why you were asked to meet us tonight. We appreciate that you agreed to come at this late hour. It's a matter of great importance. An innocent man may spend many years in jail for a crime he did not commit."

"We are counting on both of you to tell us what you know. You will not only be helping three people, Li Young, Hua, his wife, and their infant son, you will also gain the respect of the residents of both Kowloon and Hong Kong. Please tell us from the beginning what took place," Ping requested.

Jackie pointed to Jimmy to speak. As he pointed, Jackie knocked over his beer. It caused the amber liquid to seep through the teakwood cracks of the table and onto the floor. Shen bit his bottom lip. He moved his feet while a waiter rushed over to sop up the mess.

Shen promised himself that he would let the two men speak and not interrupt them. He feared they would forget an important detail. He rubbed the back of his neck and shot a glance at Ping, hoping he too would not interrupt.

Jimmy Lau spoke first. "I had the weekend shift at the Kowloon factory that week. Chang was at his station preparing his quota for the day. I had finished a conversation with him, and I was about to leave for my workstation. Jackie came by to say hello, before starting his shift. Chang was kind of smirking, you know, like someone who is hiding something. He showed us swatches he had, along with their matching labels. He took us into a storage room and showed us several rolls of material. They were standing upright in a back corner. The rolls had been placed in a large, rectangular container, bigger and deeper than a barrel. One by one, he removed the rolls. A large box rested on the bottom of the container. Chang needed help to lift the box out, so we helped him.

"After he was sure no one was near the outside door, he opened the box, exposing many rolls of a blue fabric.

Maybe eighteen or twenty rolls, all tolled. They were wrapped around clean cardboard tubing and covered in plastic. Chang was smiling."

"Then what happened?" Ping asked.

"We had never used this type of material before," Jackie interjected. "We usually sew with cottons. Chang confessed he was dealing in the underground black market, and he made his extra money this way. He said he would take a few rolls of material with each shipment that came into the factory and sell it on the black market. He said management never caught on. He told us this shipment was different. It was a fine imported silk. We had never seen or worked with it before. He knew it would bring in a higher price, so he took more than he usually would. The shipment was quite large. He asked us to join him in his lifestyle. Jimmy can tell you the rest."

"Yes," Jimmy said. Chang offered us the position of running the fabrics to the buyers. He would provide them, and we would deliver them. He said he would pay us well for our efforts." Jimmy was shaken. "Chang told us the buyers pay top prices for the stolen fabrics and sell them in the underground market for triple the price. He said the silk material would bring in an even higher price, and he would make it worth our while."

"How long has Chang been dealing with the black market," Shen asked.

Both men shook their heads. Jackie sighed. "He didn't say," Jackie answered.

"You have nothing to worry about. You have done a great service tonight. Because of both of you, we will be able to divert the case to Chang Chao being the perpetrator. We can't thank you enough." Shen said. He looked directly into their eyes. "Are you both willing to testify in court?" Shen asked. The men hesitated and gazed at each other.

The lawyers suspected some doubt. It took a bit of gentle persuasion and a promise to pick up their tab to convince Jimmy and Jackie it would be the right thing to do.

The two men had paused, but they didn't pause for long. Jimmy and Jackie simultaneously answered, "yes." The four men shook hands and left the bar.

Shen and Ping discussed the encounter they had with Chang's friends, on the way home. "We will have to drag this out for a few days. We have two witnesses that are willing to testify. I'll contact them when we get home and tell them to sit tight." Shen said.

"Let's ask for an adjourning of the court for a few days and hope the judge will allow it. We will request a meeting in Judge Ren Chow's chambers with the opposing lawyers present, and we will hope for the best." Ping replied.

"What if Jimmy and Jackie cave?" Shen asked.

"They're our only hope. If that happens the case will be over."

## CHAPTER FIFTEEN
### (Court Adjourned 1968)

The Court was already in session. It was Friday, the fourth of October, and the Wu Lawyers were running late. The Plaintiff's team was seated, and Judge Ren Chow kept checking his watch. He was angry and ready to adjourn Court for the day.

Ping Wu appeared in the doorway and hurried up the aisle. "May I approach the bench, Your Honor?"

"Go ahead, Wu, you've got exactly thirty seconds."

"Your Honor, I apologize for being late. My brother is parking the car and will be here shortly."

Chang Chao was present to give testimony. His face turned pale. He leaned in close to the Prosecutors. "What's going on?" he whispered.

One of the Kwon lawyers raised his shoulders. "I will find out right now." His face reddened. He rose and asked to approach the bench. "Your Honor, is there something we were not told? We were ready…"

"I was about to ask if both teams could meet in your chambers this morning, Your Honor," Ping interrupted. "Something new has evolved."

"In that case, I guess we'll have to talk in private," the Judge responded.

The Kwon lawyer was rattled. "Your Honor, if they have come up with something new, we should have met in your chambers before Court commenced. This is no time to spring it on us."

The Judge was angrier still. He reprimanded Ping Wu and called for a short recess.

The spectators heaved a sigh, and the Kwon family rolled their eyes and mumbled profanities.

Shen Wu appeared in the entrance doors, huffing and puffing. He ran up the aisle, apologized to the Judge, and both teams entered the Judge's chamber.

Judge Ren Chow took a seat and asked the lawyers representing Li Young to step forward. "What brings on this sudden change?" he asked.

"Your Honor, we have acquired two witnesses who are willing to testify and support Miss Nancy Sun-Ming's statements," Shen said. I apologize for this interruption of the proceedings. We received their testimony last night, at a late hour."

The prosecuting attorneys were livid. "Your Honor, we were not briefed on the two witnesses, and now they keep us waiting so they could have a good night's sleep?" one of them howled.

Judge Ren Chow raised his chin high. "Is that true, Counselor?" He waited for Shen Wu to respond.

"The two witnesses have agreed to go on the stand, whenever they are called to do so," Ping interjected.

"Are they present in the courtroom this morning?" the Judge asked.

"No, Your Honor," Ping responded.

Judge Ren Chow tilted his head up and heaved a big sigh. "I will call for an adjournment this morning. Court will resume in a few days. This will allow the attorneys to meet with the witnesses and to prepare their questions."

This was a punch in the gut for the prosecuting attorneys. However, they were thankful for the extra time to prepare and asked themselves who the Wu brothers had dug up to mess up the case. Recess was over, and they returned to the courtroom.

Judge Ren Chow returned to the bench, and the lawyers took their seats. "This Court will be adjourned until Tuesday, the eighth of October. This will give the lawyers time to present their case," he told the Court. "We will resume then."

Judge Ren Chow yelled out, "Court adjourned!" He banged the gavel so hard against the sound block, the sound resonated throughout the room and into the hallway outside.

Some spectators were bewildered, and a few were angry as they filed out of the courtroom. They wondered why they had gone in the first place.

A court officer who was on his way to a court hearing passed by several of the bystanders who had spilled out into the hallway after attending the Li Young trial. The officer was smiling and thought he was muttering under his breath, but several bystanders heard him loud and clear, "The Judge is at it again!"

<center>~~~</center>

It was Tuesday, October eighth. The Court was already in session. Jackie and Jimmy had taken seats next to Ping Wu. Judge Ren Chow was grateful he didn't have to wait for them to show up. A slow smile spread across his face.

Shen Wu stepped up to the bench and turned toward the courtroom. His eyes pointed to Jimmy. "I would like to call Jimmy Lau to the stand."

Jimmy was shaken, but he tried not to show it. His cropped straight hair was slicked back with gel. He was wearing a starched white shirt and a blue print tie. *Quite a change from the T-shirt and jeans he wore in the bar,* Shen thought.

Jimmy smiled at Judge Chow and turned his gaze toward the spectators. Chang Chao was present and seated in the first row. He gazed at his co-worker in horror. Jimmy avoided his gaze. Throughout the remainder of the day, Chang would continue to shoot daggers Jimmy's way.

The court officer asked Jimmy to raise his right hand, and he was sworn in. The questioning began.

After asking Jimmy to state his name and where he resided, Shen Wu continued. "Mr. Lau you have sworn to tell the truth. How long have you known the Defendant?"

"Since he started at the factory, Sir."

*Not that again!* Shen thought. "Can you identify him in this courtroom?"

"Yes, Sir, he's sitting in the first row." Jimmy pointed toward Li Young.

"Do you find him to be a reliable worker at your workplace?"

"Yes, I do. He's meticulous."

"Can you describe a typical workday for the sewers at the Kowloon factory?"

"Yes. We work long hours; we have to reach our quota for the day. Sometimes we work ten hours. We have two short breaks during the shift and one lunch recess. There is a short window of time before the part time shifts begin, in the early evenings. They work in a different area."

"In the time you arrive until the time you leave, have you ever observed your co-worker, Mr. Li Young, work with any materials other than the ones assigned to him?"

"No, Sir, I haven't."

"Had you ever worked with the blue silk material Mr. Young was given to make the dress shirts?"

"No. He was the only sewer in the factory to be given this new material to work with. It was special. I could tell. It was a silky fabric, shiny and slippery. To be honest, I don't think anyone else would be able to work with it. Mr. Young was the only one, in my opinion, who could."

"Doesn't that prove he had the opportunity to steal the fabrics?" The Kwon lawyer stood as he shouted. "The labels were found at his workstation." He glanced at the jurors' faces, hoping for a reaction. There was none. Judge Ren Chow was infuriated.

"It's not your turn Counselor, you'll have a chance to question the witness. Let's hear the testimony and find out what he has to say, and if there's another outburst like this one, I will hold you in contempt of court." Judge Ren Chow nodded his head as his eyes pointed to Shen Wu. "Proceed."

"Mr. Lau, did you ever see the Defendant with the blue silk fabric at any other time, except when using it at his sewing machine to make the shirts?"

"No, Sir."

"Have you ever seen him with the swatches or labels for that same fabric?"

"No, Sir, never!"

"What is your relationship with your co-worker, Chang Chao?"

"We are friends, or at least we *were* friends." Jimmy avoided Chang's eyes. Waves of laughter erupted from the spectators.

Shen Wu continued with the questioning. "Can you identify him? Is he present in this courtroom today?"

"Yes, Sir, he's seated over there," Jimmy said, pointing to Chang Chao.

"Would you say you were close enough of a friend that he would ask you to do something against your principles?"

"Objection," the Chief Prosecutor cried. "That's a leading question."

"Objection overruled. Answer the question," the Judge ordered. He did not take his eyes off of Jimmy.

"I think so, in fact he did." Jimmy answered.

"What do you mean, 'he did.'" Shen asked.

"One day, me and my friend Jackie Yuan arrived to work early. Chang Chao was at his workstation. We greeted him and had some small talk. He was grinning, so we asked him what the joke was. He showed us the swatches and the designer labels from a new shipment that had come in recently. We knew…"

"Objection, Your Honor," the Prosecuting Attorney interrupted. "He's insinuating the other witness has corroborated his story."

"Objection sustained, strike that from the record," the Judge ordered. The Court stenographer nodded. Judge Ren Chow pointed his index finger at Jimmy. "Continue Mr. Lau."

"Sorry, Your Honor. *I* knew Chang would not have been given that material to work with, so I asked him where he got the swatches from."

"Was your co-worker, Mr. Jackie Yuan, present at the time?" Shen asked.

"Yes, he was standing next to me."

"What happened next?"

"Chang Chao asked if we would like to see something in the back room. I told him I would. Jackie followed. He took us into a storeroom and lifted bolts of fabric out of a large box-like container. Under the materials, there laid a long cardboard box. It was heavy, so we helped him lift it. He opened the box and showed us the silk fabrics. The silks were on heavy cardboard cylinders, each wrapped in thick plastic. I didn't understand why they would be in his possession. He approached us and asked us if we would be willing to make trips with this fabric and other fabrics. He whispered he was connected to the black market in Hong Kong, and if we chose to run them to the buyers, it would be profitable for us."

"That's all the questioning for today, Mr. Lau."

"You may step down, Mr. Lau." Judge Ren Chow ordered.

The courtroom was in an uproar. People talking and shouting at the same time. Some were excited, some confused, and others who knew Chang were not surprised.

The Plaintiff's legal team was enraged. Chang Chao sat in silence. He remained aghast that his co-worker would expose him for what he was, a thief and a liar; lying to the extent he would send an innocent man to jail for many years.

The reporters in the back of the courtroom ran out, bumping into each other as they ran, each one trying to be the first to make the deadline.

Reporter, Sky Wong, had left when Jimmy gave the last word of his testimony. Once again, his byline would make the early edition of the Tin Tin Daily.

Li Young could not hold back the tears. His wife Hua was not there to hear Jimmy's testimony, but she remained hopeful. Chang's panic set in, and Judge Ren Chow adjourned the court session until Wednesday, October ninth, at 9:00 a.m., "sharp!"

~~~

On Wednesday, October ninth, the trial commenced. Ping Wu was doing the questioning. He called Chang's co-worker, Jackie Yuan, to the stand. He was dressed in neat trousers and a white starched shirt. His tie was red and blue plaid, and his black hair remained tied back in a pony tail. He looked like a young boy about to start his first day of primary school. His statements were precise and articulate, corroborating every word of Jimmy's testimony.

The prosecuting attorneys could not discredit a word of the testimony of either witness, although they tried. Nor could they get either witness to agree with one issue they had conjured up to cause an iota of doubt.

Shen and Ping Wu's long shot had won!

The court case went on for several days. Chang Chao could not return to the Kowloon factory until the case was resolved, and he was unable to get rid of the evidence. At the Kwan family's request, a search warrant had been issued, and the box of silk fabrics was found in the container, just as Jimmy Lau and Jackie Yuan had testified.

Forensics was called in, and they were able to match Chang's fingerprints with the prints on not only the box of fabrics but also on the fabric labels.

The Tin Tin Daily had a field day! Sky Wong's byline read: FACTORY WORKER EXONERATED OF ROBBERY. It went on to say, Chang Chao, a worker at the Kowloon factory, was connected with the garment workers black market, and he was charged with the crime.

Chang Chao was dismissed immediately from his job at the Kowloon factory and convicted of robbery. He was being held in custody; His sentence is still pending.

## CHAPTER SIXTEEN
### (The Shunem Woman 2001)

The fall season brought an array of color to paint the Camwood landscape. The swamp maples had already turned a golden yellow, standing out among the many species of trees that dotted the village. Sprays of burnt orange, vermilion, and crimson were splattered here and there to complete the Master's canvas. The spectacular vistas provided a panorama that drew many students to the small town. Just a stone's throw from a prestigious ivy league college, many students piled into the town, like crowds into a store on Black Friday.

On the weekends, students were known to frequent restaurants and bars in the area, attend live theatre shows and hang out in the parks. From twilight until the sun peeked over the horizon, they enjoyed the musicians that offered whatever talents they had. When the street lamps went out, they retreated to their dorms.

Chen was hoping with the influx of visitors Camwood would welcome, some would stop by his Church. His heart's desire was to reach the younger generation, one that seemed to be falling away from true worship. He had been part of that world until he met Niki. Why had she stuck by him, knowing his way of life? He wondered. Was it she had seen something in him only God saw? He had become her knight in shining armor, and he never understood why. Having faith, she waited, and he was glad. One day he would tell his story—the story of how the Lord delivered him from

the lifestyle he had chosen. He would save that for another
time.

~~~

Chen's services had gone well. He had delivered his sermons
to a congregation that seemed to grasp most of what he was
trying to convey. God is a forgiving God. We need only to
repent and accept His Son's atonement for sin, by the
shedding of His Blood on the cross. Sinners are  reconciled
to a Holy God. They are forgiven. The gift is free!

~~~

As he sat in his study Chen leaned back in his green leather
wing chair. He closed his eyes and thought back to his first
sermon. The day had been overcast. The warm glow that
usually saturated the sanctuary was nowhere to be found.

Chen had no trouble telling the congregation how
much of an asset Samuel had been to him. Samuel had sat in
the first row, during the service. He heard the accolades and
smiled from ear to ear. His mother, Jeanette, sat beside him.
By the time Chen was done with his narrative, the entire
church body embraced Samuel as one of their own. Thoughts
of Samuel always made Chen smile.

Chen had stood at the church's door afterwards to
greet the new congregants and share a word or two. Many
complimented him on his sermon and how inviting the
sanctuary looked.

Another image came to Chen's mind. It was as clear
as the crystal waters that ran over the rocks in the stream
beyond the parsonage. It was the day he and Niki would
receive a visit from a stranger that would change their lives
forever.

Chen's eyes remained closed as he continued to
reminisce.

~~~

The sounds of a distant chorus whistling through the
woodland pines had awakened Niki before sunrise. The
many species of birds that inhabited the woodlands seemed

to have joined in unison to announce the new day. Each morning they would congregate in the meadow beyond the parsonage, and they would await their turn for a meal. The ritual continued as the sun peeked over the Green Mountains, leaving a tangerine sky. It swiftly moved higher in the heavens. Niki rose and went downstairs to prepare breakfast. It was June 2001.

After breakfast, Niki and Chen hurried upstairs to dress for Sunday morning service.

By 9:30 a.m., the sanctuary was full. People were piling in for the 10:00 a.m. service. Chen was looking out at the sanctuary and thought he had better speak to someone about extending the space. He made a mental note to call a friend during the coming week.

Niki sat in front to the left of the pulpit. She remained a bit nervous and blamed it on the two cups of coffee she had consumed earlier.

Chen's sermon that week would be on God's provision. He would base it on the biblical story of Elisha and the Shunammite woman.

"Elisha would go to a town called Shunem, on occasion," Chen told his congregation. "Each time Elisha went he would pass a woman's house. She watched him as he passed and recognized he was a man of God—a prophet.

"One day she asked her husband if she could give him a meal. He agreed. After that, each time the prophet came through the town, the woman would prepare a meal for him. After a time, she asked her husband if she could make a room on the roof of their house for him to stay in whenever he came to town. Her husband agreed. It's what she put in the room for his comfort that intrigued me," Chen said.

Chen looked about the sanctuary to see if anyone showed interest in what he was saying. One congregant was yawning, and another was whispering to his wife. A third, Mrs. Brandywine, kept her head down, and he couldn't tell if she was reading the bible she had placed in her lap or she had fallen asleep. Several children in the back of the sanctuary were talking loudly. They refused to attend Sunday School and opted to stay with their parents.

Chen motioned with his hands to the man in charge of the sound system to raise the volume. Chen spoke a bit louder, and Mrs. Brandywine jumped as if she had sat on a pine cone. Chen, who had not taken his eyes off her, stifled a laugh, but not before a chuckle escaped his lips.

"You would think when decorating a guest room for our friends or relatives, we would go to extremes to make it beautiful and choose the finest furniture and accessories. But this woman from Shunem only chose four items for Elisha to make him feel at home. She was a wealthy woman, so it wasn't a matter of not being able to afford the best."

Chen went on to ask the congregation: "Does anyone know what these four items were?" There was no response. He remained quiet for a few seconds to give the congregants a chance to think.

A small voice in the back of the church shouted out, "I know one item; it was a chair."

"That's right." Chen answered. Had she guessed? "Scripture tells us the four items were a bed, a table, a chair, and a lamp. Do any of you think when preparing a room for a guest you would provide only these four items and nothing else? Not even a picture on the wall? I think not. But you see, Brothers and Sisters, the Shunammite woman was providing this man of God with everything he would need for his comfort, and nothing more!

"If you think it wasn't enough for him, let's break down the four items and see the significance of them. First of all, she provided a bed for him. She knew he would be weary from his travels. A bed would provide rest and peace. The next item she provided him with was a table. A table represents God's provision. His Word tells us: 'And my God will supply all your needs according to His riches in glory in Christ Jesus.'" "The 23rd Psalm reminds us, 'You prepare a table before me in the presence of my enemies.'" "God always provides for his children," he added.

"The third item was a chair." Chen said. He looked at the woman who shouted out before, and he smiled. "Can anyone tell me what a chair would represent to the Shunem woman?" No one raised their hand. "I will tell you. A chair represents authority! Jesus has given us authority to act in His name. Many of us are timid and shy when it comes to taking authority over the enemy. We have the power to tell the devil to flee in Jesus' name."

Chen looked about the room. Heads went up, and people were starting to pay attention. "Lastly, the Shunem woman provided him with a lamp. To her the lamp stood for revelation. Revelation consists of the wisdom to recognize it is a revelation from God and the understanding of how God wants you to use this knowledge He has given you. You must pray.

"Jesus, the Messiah Who came and will return, is the lamp. He's the light of the world. Darkness and light cannot stay in the same room. When you enter a room, you switch on the light, and the darkness flees, it no longer exists. If you leave and switch the light off, the darkness returns. But Jesus' light is eternal. It never goes out. So, the woman from Shunem was giving Elisha everything he needed, as God does for us. It's not about what we want or think we need. God's provision is *all* we need. He will never sell us short."

Everyone had gone from the church. Chen felt he had touched a few souls. Several congregants had stopped by to tell him, and he was grateful. Niki left for the parsonage to rest, and Chen returned to his office.

Chen was keeping a file on his sermons and the references he used to write them. As he was placing his sermon into the folder, he heard a faint knock on the door. He looked up to see a young girl in the doorway. He invited her in and asked her to sit. He excused himself for a few moments and entered the hallway to summon his wife.

Niki appeared in a matter of minutes. They walked into the office together to find the girl in tears. Niki pulled over a chair and sat next to her. She took the girl's hand and held it. "When you are ready to speak to us, we are ready to listen," Chen said.

The girl said her name was Marcie Evans. She explained she had no one to turn to, and she had heard Chen's sermon. Would the Lord provide for her as he had preached?

"Why don't you tell us what your problem is, Marcie?" Chen asked.

Marcie looked into Chen's eyes. She was silent. Niki squeezed her hand. "Go on, you have nothing here to fear, nor will anything you tell us leave this room without your permission. Please continue."

Marcie brushed the tears away. "How old are you?" Chen asked.

"I'm sixteen."

"Are you ready to tell us what's bothering you?"

"I'm pregnant," Marcie responded. Her body was trembling, and she covered her face with her hands and began to sob.

Niki took Marcie's hands and held them tighter. "Have you told your parents?"

"My mother knows. I couldn't bring myself to tell my dad. When she finally told him, he kicked me out of the house. When I passed the church today, I heard the most beautiful singing. It comforted me. I stepped inside and listened from the vestibule. Your sermon made me think. God will provide for me. He will take care of me and my baby. My dad said if I didn't get an abortion, I must leave."

"Where are you staying," Chen asked.

"I went to the local shelter. I didn't know what else to do. I've been there a few weeks."

Niki shot a glance at Chen, wanting his approval. She didn't wait long. "You can stay with us until we figure this out," Niki offered. Chen smiled.

Marcie threw her arms around Niki. "I'm afraid. I don't want to have an abortion," she cried. "I want to keep my baby."

Chen was moved and angered at the same time. He couldn't understand why, when Marcie needed them the most, her parents would not help her. "Of course, you can stay with us! Like the Shunammite woman's guest room, our spare room is sparse, but we will try and meet your needs."

"Are you ready to tell us who the father is?" Chen asked.

"He's a boy from school. He's seventeen. He had been asking me to go out with him for a long time. He was not my type. He smoked marijuana, and I know he was drinking on the weekends.

"One day he grabbed me in the hallway during change of classes. He pushed me into the janitors' closet and blocked the door. He tried to kiss me. I slapped his face, and I started to yell out. He covered my mouth and pulled me down. He's a big guy—strong. He's on the wrestling team."

Marcie stopped for a moment, and her eyes swelled up with tears. "He kept one hand over my mouth and tore my clothes with the other hand. I could barely breathe. He raped me and left me on the floor. I was hysterical. He told me no one would believe me if I told on him. He said his father had power. I stayed in that closet until school was out. I was crying, and I looked terrible. My blouse was ripped, and my jeans were dirty from the floor. I walked home alone."

"What happened when you reached your home?" Chen asked.

"My parents weren't home. I took a shower and changed my clothes. I threw the clothes I was wearing at school in the trash can outside. My mother came home first.

I was afraid to tell her." She paused. She could no longer go on speaking.

"Take your time," Niki said. She rose and went over to the water cooler near the entrance door. She poured a cup of the cold liquid and handed it to Marcie.

Marcie took the cup and thanked her. She sipped the water, and after composing herself, she continued. "When I found out I was pregnant, I told my mother what happened at school. I don't think she believed me. Later on, she told my dad I was raped. The only thing my dad said to her was 'she better not get pregnant,' he never did console me," Marcie cried. "When he found out I *was* pregnant, he kicked me out. I wanted to go to the police, but I couldn't bring myself to do it. You are the only ones, besides my parents, who know what happened."

"Will you tell us who he is?" Chen asked.

"I'm not ready to do that! His dad is a politician and probably has connections. I can't fight them."

"We will deal with the boy later," Chen said. "For now, let's get some food into you. A hot meal and a good night's rest will do you good."

That evening as they climbed the stairs leading to the guest room, the couple continued to comfort Marcie, and Niki felt Chen had encountered his first challenge as a Pastor.

Chen's images faded.

## CHAPTER SEVENTEEN
(A Farewell 1984)

It was June 1984. The Hong Kong rainy season was in full swing. Chen had completed his last semester of upper secondary school. His parents, Li and Hua, had saved enough money to send him to his uncle and aunt's home in the northeastern part of the United States. Chen was looking forward to a new life in another world.

It rained almost every day with the threat of a typhoon lingering over the island. As traffic diminished, light raincoats and umbrellas were the fashion. On some days, people from different walks of life were confined to their homes. Merchants, restaurant workers, bankers, and professionals all stayed home.

The weather remained warm, and the downpours became dangerous. Manholes flooded, and anchored cables came unhinged. The economy suffered a bit, but the people of Hong Kong were used to it.

Chen had done well in school. His father's brother, Benny, and his wife, Joy, kept in touch. They were helping Chen decide where he would like to attend college in the States. His desire was to work in law enforcement, and his major would be Criminal Justice. He hoped to learn all he could and one day share his knowledge with his friends in Hong Kong.

~~~

Hua arose early to prepare a special breakfast for Chen of satay beef on a roll with milk tea. It was the day he would migrate to the United States. It was the day Li and Hua had saved for all those years, hoping to give their son a better life.

Chen was excited, yet fear of the unknown was setting in. He wanted to spend some time alone in his room.

Chen sat on his bed and stared at the images on the wall—images which had evolved through the years. His friends stared back at him. Memories rushed through his mind, like the shutter on his camera, one click at a time. There were recollections of weekend excursions, walks on the pier, and his first date. There were memories of friends he had gone to concerts with and attended festivals with, where they ate all night and found their way to the central part of the city to eye the young girls. He reminisced about bike rides to Quarry Bay Park and picnic lunches under a Banyan tree, its roots growing down and its branches spread out like a tiny forest. There were school dances, fishing trips, and car rides with some boys whose parents were well off and could afford a car of their own.

One of Chen's final thoughts went to his first love. Her name was Jovi Song.

~~~

It had rained that weekend. Chen and his friends were looking for something to do. They decided to ride to where they believed the action was. The teens were disappointed, most people had stayed home.

The splattering of rain on the roofs of Hong Kong had morphed into a torrent. Their night of lying about their age and getting into a bar for a few drinks became a pipe dream. Not one of them looked a day older than sixteen.

The rain continued to hit the roofs, like pellets from an air rifle. The boys decided to duck into a nearby bowling alley. The sound of the resin balls hitting the pins as they glided down the smooth as glass alleys, beckoned them to stay.

The boys approached the main desk. They had pooled their money together and rented four bowling balls.

The shoes they would need were slick to help them slide as they hurled the balls down the polished lanes. They were made of leather with rubber soles to provide traction when needed. They were supplied to them as a courtesy of the management.

The teens took alley number 13. There were four girls on alley 14, and Chen and his buddies couldn't help but watch them play. They were sure the girls would make fools of themselves. The four boys stood and crossed their arms. They watched the girls bowl from the corner of their eyes, all four sporting crooked half-smiles. One of the girls caught the look. She turned and faced the boys. She mirrored their smile, stepped up to lane 14 and hurled the ball down the alley. It landed a perfect strike! She turned back facing the boys and crossed her arms.

Chen was impressed. Their cheeks tinged with red, his buddies' faces told their story. Chen was taken in by her and knew he had to find out who she was.

The teens played for about an hour, their shadows projected onto the glossy bowling lane. After they exhausted their time, Chen walked toward the girls. There were four, which made it easier for the boys, but Chen made it clear to his friends that the champion bowler was his. "Hi, I'm Chen," he smiled as he approached her.

"My name is Jovi—Jovi Song." "I noticed you were laughing at us. Are you still laughing now?" she added.

Chen smiled. "No, you showed us a thing or two! How about meeting us for ice cream sodas next door?" he asked. "I want to find out who this Jovi Song is." His voice, as soft as velvet, was barely heard by Jovi.

Jovi, too, was taken with Chen. She loved the way he carried himself, despite his shyness. She appreciated his dark eyes and his tied back long, shiny hair. He seemed different than any other boy in Hong Kong. She also noticed his pristine white teeth which told her he wasn't a smoker.

Jovi stood about five foot one. Her silky black hair appeared shorter as it turned under at the nape of her neck. Chen was attracted to her small frame. She was dressed in a solid royal blue dress that cut off at the knees, its color enhancing her large dark eyes.

Jovi and her friends agreed to meet at the ice cream shop. They spent the better part of the night sharing stories about their life on the island. Chen felt comfortable with Jovi and decided to take a chance and ask her for a date.

Jovi agreed to meet Chen the following Saturday night. They would meet at a skating rink, not far from the bowling alley. The other boys hadn't faired so well. They opted out.

~~~

The following weekend, the two met as planned. They chose an indoor rink in the central part of the city. Chen arranged a ride from the father of one of his friends. He would meet Jovi at the rink at 7:00 p.m. His friend's father would return at 11:00 p.m. to pick him up. Jovi's family dropped her off and arranged to pick her up at the same time Chen would be leaving.

The rink was massive. Its skating arena took up most of the space. One side of the building had floor to ceiling windows, overlooking midtown from the second level. There were huge gray columns covered in green and purple florescent lighting that pulsated to the rhythm of the music, and there were several balconies overhead that housed the management offices, allowing the skaters to be observed by those working above.

Chen paid for Jovi's skates, and they skated until the music stopped at 11:00 p.m. Neither of them were proficient skaters, but neither of them fell. It was obvious they just wanted to be together.

"I really had a great time," Jovi exclaimed.

"Me too!" Chen smiled.

"Chen, I have to tell you something. I leave for London this summer. I'm staying with my cousin Kim and her family. We will be attending Cambridge University next fall. Maybe you and I could write to each other, I would like that."

Chen was taken aback. His thoughts of having a girlfriend had played in his mind all week. He imagined taking her all sorts of places, like the Hong Kong Zoo and the Botanical Gardens. He dreamed of taking long walks down at the Quarry Bay pier promenade, and there would be strolls through Chater Garden. His dreams were being shattered; he was crushed. The relationship was over before it had even begun.

Chen replied softly, "I understand. Yes, Jovi, I will remember to write whenever you get settled, and I wish you well at school."

The teens did write for a while. But before the second college semester was completed, Jovi's letters stopped.

Chen was resigned that Jovi had found a new love, and one day he would find love also—but it wouldn't be with Jovi Song. How many others have had the same experience? Chen wondered. It took several years before Jovi's image faded from his mind.

~~~

Chen continued to stare at the wall in his room. The images were of his secondary school buddies. They had hung together since primary school. They were of different faiths; several were Buddhists, and several had grown up in Christian homes. Chen would attend church with the Christian boys from time to time. He did it for no special reason, except to have something to do. At his young age, he was not searching.

"Time to leave, Chen," Hua called out. We have been offered a ride to the airport. The Nguyens from Kowloon Tong will take us. You don't want to miss your plane."

~~~

The ride to the airport was painful for both Chen and his parents. He was now seventeen and would soon become a man. He had excelled in his studies and graduated earlier than expected. His parents had instilled in him a work ethic that would make any parent proud. They knew he would succeed in America.

The family arrived at Kai Tak International Airport an hour before boarding. It was located east of Kowloon Bay and surrounded on three sides by water. There were rugged mountains to the north, some reaching an elevation of two thousand feet which made landings difficult. His parents used the extra time to give advice and warnings they felt would help him in the decisions he would have to make.

They embraced and said their final goodbyes. Hua cried, and Li tried hard not to show emotion. Chen had no trouble as tears flowed heavily down both cheeks, landing on his starched white shirt collar.

Chen thanked the Nguyens and bid them goodbye. His parents watched as he boarded the plane with a final wave. Chen was unaware it would be thirteen years before his parents would join him in America.

## CHAPTER EIGHTEEN
(A New Adventure 1984)

Chen's plane landed at 5 p.m., New York time. Midway, there was one stopover. After over seventeen hours of traveling, he was exhausted. He tried to sleep while in the air, but the excitement mixed with fear was too much for him.

He lifted his carry-on luggage from the overhead compartment, as the captains's voice bellowed over the loudspeaker. "Welcome to New York's John F. Kennedy Airport. Enjoy your stay. Please check your seats and make sure you leave nothing behind. Thank you for flying Cathay Pacific." That was it!

Chen waited his turn to descend the steps of the plane onto the tarmac. He went directly to baggage claim. He recognized his suitcase and lifted it from the carousel. As he entered the visitors' area, his uncle and aunt were waiting. They were both holding up a large sign, welcoming him to America. He could not help but notice as it bobbed up and down above the heads of the crowd.

His aunt, Joy, ran to him smiling. She threw her arms around Chen speaking something in Cantonese. His uncle, Benny, approached him, and a strong hug followed. "Fun jing," his uncle repeated over and over, as he patted him on the shoulder.

The ride to their home was fascinating for Chen. He was amazed at the wide roads and the trees that lined the parkways. He was picked up in a shiny, new white Ford

Mustang convertible. Its black top was protected from the elements of sun and rain with a red canvas covering when not in use. It was pristine. Chen was speechless.

Chen's uncle, Benny, was a wealthy businessman. Since his arrival in the United States, he became an exporter of cars to the Orient. He had worked in the sales department at first. Years later, when his boss retired, he was able to buy the business. His net worth was in the millions.

Benny was a generous man, never forgetting the poverty he came from. He wanted to share his wealth with his nephew, and if Chen was willing to move to the States he had offered to send him to the best of schools. His dream for his nephew had now become a reality.

~~~

Benny's home was palatial. It was a large Dutch colonial in the upper crust areas of the suburbs. It was situated on seven acres of land.

As he entered the house, Chen stopped to take in the luxury before him. There was a staircase to his left, leading to the second level. It winded in a graceful curve. It was covered in a traditional red and blue paisley pattern, made of thick wool. Chen could tell the staircase had been custom built, most likely by a local craftsman. It had a large oak pedestal and banister. The balusters were painted white, and the treads were solid oak.

On the right of the staircase was a large living area. It housed a stacked stone fireplace that was centered on the far wall. There were two blue corduroy chairs flanking it on either side. Chen noticed the different shades and various sizes of the stones that made the fireplace a striking focal point in the room. Immediately, he sensed the coziness and warmth they created. The hearth was decorated in small ceramic tiles of various colors. In one corner of the hearth was a brass holder that held a small broom, a shovel and a poker. Chen took it all in. He was impressed; The room was timeless.

A large beveled mirror, its trim painted in gold leaf, hung gracefully over a hand carved mantel. The mantel was crafted in solid chestnut. "This hardwood came from an old farm before the infestation of fungus that took place in the late nineteenth century," Benny explained. "It nearly wiped out the entire species of chestnut trees."

Chen admired the deep chocolate shade of the wood. "A true artist carved this, and he fashioned it into a work of art," he offered.

"You are right," Benny responded, excited that his nephew recognized its value.

Chen approached the mantel. It held many family photos, each one framed in gold. He smiled as he lifted one of the frames that held an image of his parents, but the other images were unfamiliar to him. He stood still and quiet as he saw his mother and father smiling back. For a moment, he felt numb. He placed the frame back gently onto the mantel. His uncle caught his expression. "Let me show you my study," Benny said. He ushered Chen into the hallway.

Chen admired the built-in shelves that encircled the room as they stepped into the study. They were stacked with hundreds of books. After he settled in Chen would ask his uncle and aunt which books they would recommend for him to read.

Beyond the hallway was a large kitchen. It was equipped with several state-of-the-art appliances and a porcelain sink. The cabinets were made of solid maple, with brass hardware and pulls, and the floor was a blue and green pattern of slate that had been rubbed with teak oil.

As the men entered the kitchen, Chen noticed the pungent odor of linseed oil. Benny explained that the cabinets had been recently treated. He insisted on treating his household possessions organically, rather than buying commercial products, and it showed in the natural shine of the furniture and flooring. Although the linseed oil had been boiled before using it, the odor would linger for several weeks until it cured. Benny made no apologies for it. Things had to be done his way.

A corridor led to a foyer and back door. The yard was beyond it. It was covered in thick grass, as smooth as jade, with a garden sectioned off. In the middle of the garden stood a fountain made of cast stone. It was surrounded by orange, red, and white New Guinea impatiens. Chen thought it resembled a post card.

There were white wicker chairs and tables scattered throughout the yard. They were placed in shady spots to accommodate Benny's guests and those who liked to read outdoors.

Benny was looking forward to planting various kinds of fruit trees on the land and had researched the many varieties of fruit that would grow well in the New England climate. Spring would be the best time for planting, and he envisioned the abundance of apples, peaches, plums, and figs they would produce.

A bar-b-que pit was built into the ground with wooden Adirondack chairs circling it. Chen thought of the many weekends they must have celebrated there. How many friends must have gathered on holidays and special occasions. Chen pictured it all.

There was a horse stable, not far from the main house. It housed two riding horses, Lilly and Lotus. Lilly was white with black patches on her sides, and Lotus was brown with a tan mane and white hoofs. The horses and stalls were cared for by a man named Tom Green.

Chen's Uncle Benny suggested they take a short walk before dinner. He wanted to introduce his nephew to Tom and the horses. His wife, Joy, stayed behind.

As they approached the stable, Tom was brushing Lotus. He smiled and greeted Benny and Chen. Benny introduced Chen to Tom and invited him to come and join them for dinner, but he declined. "I still have to feed the horses and bed them down for the night. Maybe another time, if that's all right with you?"

Tom took some time to show Chen the stable and the surrounding trails. "Maybe in your spare time we could take a ride around the property. Come down anytime, I'm usually here."

Chen and Benny walked back to the house, and Chen imagined he might have found his first friend in America.

~~~

Tom Green was a dedicated caretaker. He was known for his passion for horses and his patience in caring for them. He was always raising the bar, learning all he could, aspiring one day to have horses of his own. He was on the stout side and extremely shy. His chestnut hair was of a medium length, and he preferred an unshaven face, hiding his timidity behind his bristly stubble. Tom didn't socialize much and spent most of his time at the Young's estate, having settled in a small cottage on the premises. He was unmarried, with no regrets.

Impressed with his knowledge, Chen would look to Tom as a mentor of sorts. Chen would help with the stable chores, in his spare time, and they would spend many hours on the weekends having deep conversations about their aspirations and goals. Lilly would become his favorite horse, and he would ride her often through the surrounding woodlands and riding trails nearby.

~~~

After dinner the couple showed Chen his room. It would be his hangout for the next few years while he attended college. The Police Academy would follow.

Chen's room was large with two windows on the south wall and one window on the north, enough for lots of sunshine and fresh air to come through. A twin bed rested against the west wall. It had an antique bird's-eye maple nightstand at its side. Chen's uncle, Benny, was delighted when Chen recognized the rarity of the wood.

There was a desk made of cherrywood that stood in one corner of the room. A tall lamp rested on it. It had a gold metal shade, like the lamps in some of the fancier libraries in America. A brown leather swivel chair was tucked into the knee hole of the desk. A phone lay on its green felt top.

There were built-in bookcases made from mahogany wood with plenty of space to start his own library. It was his uncle's wish Chen fill it.

There was a private bathroom with a tub and shower, next to his bedroom. Chen was overwhelmed.

Chen asked if he could be excused for the night. He had a lot to think about, and he wanted to unwind in his room. His day had come to an end.

Not taking anything for granted, Chen appreciated that his uncle had to work hard to get where he was in life. Benny's example encouraged him to do the same. He knew his Uncle Benny had achieved his wealth with sweat and tears. Chen also knew Benny was a humble man, never bragging of his accomplishments but always trying to teach and encourage Chen to reach his goals. Chen was thankful, but the guilt of leaving his parents behind haunted him.

As Chen lay on his bed, he thought of all he had seen and experienced this day. He surmised his parents were struggling at home in Hong Kong. It was then he vowed to work hard, save every penny and send for them.

## CHAPTER NINETEEN
(Samuel and the Lamb)

December 2001 was ushered in with frigid temperatures. Camwood's lakes and smaller streams froze. Many tourists decided to stay home. The only boost the economy had in the small town was brought in with the younger crowd who attended the ivy league college nearby. The popular winter sports had trickled down to ice skating on the lakes that were deemed safe.

Chen was busy tending to his congregants, and Niki was busy tending to Marcie. The baby was due in a few weeks, and they were prepared to greet the new arrival with joy.

Samuel was back attending school and looking forward to the winter break when he could help out at the church and have short visits with Marcie.

After an early breakfast, Chen entered the sanctuary. The colored panes of the arched windows filtered the winter sun, casting a golden glow about the room.

Chen smiled when he noticed Samuel seated on one of the church benches, but his smile diminished when he saw that Samuel looked disturbed.

"What can I do for you today, Samuel?"

"I'm having a hard time with the students at school again." Samuel replied.

"Did you skip school today because of it?"

"Oh no! It's teachers' meetings today, we have off."

"Samuel," Chen responded with a look of concern, "do you have a minute, I'd like to share something with you."

"Sure, Pastor."

Chen sat beside Samuel. "Samuel, there will always be people in your life, in all of our lives, who will treat us unkindly. Even if it's through no fault of our own. We have to forgive them. God expects us to," he said.

"What do you mean?"

"Samuel, we have all sinned in some way, and when we *do* sin, we want God's forgiveness, right?"

"Yes."

"I know it's hard to pray for someone who has hurt you, but if you bring it to the Lord, He will help you get through it. You only need to tell Him; He's always ready to listen."

Samuel stared at his hands. "I tried that, Pastor, it don't work."

"Most accounts we read in the bible are true happenings," Chen continued, "but sometimes Jesus would tell a parable to bring out a point."

"What's a parable?"

"A parable is a story. Its purpose is to give the person you are telling it to a clear image of what you are trying to teach them."

"Can you tell me one?"

"Yes, I can. This one tells how unkind some people can be to others. It can be found in a book of the Old Testament. I feel God wants me to tell you this story because the book I'm speaking of is the book of Samuel." Chen smiled. "What do you think of that?"

"I think its fine," Samuel answered. He smiled back with a wide grin, exposing his white teeth that were now covered in silver braces.

Chen continued with his narrative. "There was a rich man who owned a great number of sheep and cattle. There was also a poor man who had no worldly possessions, except this little ewe lamb he had bought. He loved the lamb, and he raised it with his children. It ate at his table and shared his food. It drank from his cup, and he treated it as if it were a member of his family, like you treat Archie!" "One day a traveler came to visit the rich man. Instead of taking one of the many lambs from his own flock to make a meal with, he took the poor man's pet lamb, killed it, and he served it to the visitor."

Samuel was devastated. He thought of his pet dog, Archie. He remained quiet for a few seconds. He bit his bottom lip. "If anyone did that to Archie, I would kill him!"

Chen took a handkerchief from his breast pocket and wiped a tear from the corner of Samuel's eye. "Samuel, that's not God's way. And knowing you, I doubt you *would* do that. Listen! If the rich man repented, if he was really sorry for what he had done, would God forgive him?"

"Yes."

"Like you and me when we sin. Many of us have been unkind in the past, in one way or another; most times without meaning to. If we told God we were truly sorry, we would expect Him to forgive us, wouldn't we?"

"What happened after?" Samuel asked. "Did the poor man forgive the rich man?"

"I don't know Samuel the scripture doesn't tell us. But I would like to think he did because that's what God says we should do—forgive."

Chen paused, to give Samuel time to think about what he was trying to convey to him. He could tell Samuel was having a hard time dealing with forgiving an unkindness.

Chen continued. "Samuel, the prophet Nathan was telling this story to someone in order to make a point. You see the rich man showed no pity on the poor man because he didn't have a close relationship with God. If he had, the man would never have planned such an evil deed. They both showed by their actions their true character. You are someone of character, and you *do* have a close relationship with the Lord. When these mean kids approach you at school and say harmful things to you, try to remember they need a closer relationship with God, and you should pray for them. You should speak to your teachers and the social worker at school. They are there to help. You should also let your mother know what's bothering you."

"I hope the rich man bought the poor man another lamb!" Samuel reached the sanctuary door. He turned and looked at Chen. "Did God know I would be called Samuel?"

Chen smiled. "I know He did!"

Chen made a mental note to call Samuel's mom. He would let Jeanette know of his issue at school.

Samuel's eyes twinkled. He thanked the pastor for the story and left the sanctuary satisfied.

## CHAPTER TWENTY
### (The Bouquet - Winter 2001)

In the months following Marcie's moving in with the Youngs, her parents had not tried to find her, yet she was peaceful. She felt God had placed her in a loving home, and she would be forever grateful to the Young family. Marcie was further along in her pregnancy, and her tiny frame revealed it.

Niki had made all of Marcie's maternity outfits, using gingham and seersucker fabrics for the warmer months and heavier cottons and tweeds as the weather turned colder. Marcie alternated wearing them, laundering them between changes. She helped with the church and the parsonage, and she did a bit of light cleaning. She also accompanied Niki to town on shopping days.

Niki was unable to conceive. The doctors she had seen made it clear to her. To have a baby in the house would be a joy and a blessing to her and Chen. She thanked God every day for the opportunity to be part of the baby's life.

Before they established a friendship, Marcie had seen Samuel from time to time hanging around the school yard. He was always alone. Samuel knew he was different, and he had learned to accept his disabilities. He was developing a man's body, yet his mind had not caught up with it? Why couldn't the world see him as his mother, Jeanette, or Chen, or Niki, or even Marcie saw him? He wondered.

~~~

Samuel had finished his chores at the church and stopped by Chen's office. "Would I be able to visit Marcie today?" he asked.

"Go ahead, Samuel. Don't stay too long, okay?" Chen smiled as he watched Samuel leave and head for the rear door. He had a spring in his step.

The church garden was situated behind the parsonage. There was a pebbled path leading to it from the back door. On a sunny day, sparkles of color encased in the small stones would glisten like the sequins on a bridal gown.

The path was surrounded by gray blocks of stone, laid without mortar nearly a century before. Beyond the garden was a meadow, surrounded by woodlands. Beyond the woodlands a wide stream flowed, abundant in brook trout and bass, born from a gift the surrounding mountains always seemed to provide. Its crystal-clear water flowed gently, running over the rocks and stones and emptying into a river a few miles east of the church.

During the spring, summer, and fall months, the garden and meadow were always abundant in an array of different hues and shades. The colorful daylilies, the pink astilbe, with their tall plumes and lacy foliage and the many varieties of geraniums that had complimented the peonies of red, coral, and white were long gone.

The fragrant shrubs of lavender, the garden phlox, and the giant blooms of blue and purple hydrangeas, all trimmed with a ground cover of creeping thyme had also disappeared along with the purple chicory and white bonesets that graced the fall, their long, narrow leaves sticking out from the sandy soil. It was now winter!

Samuel eyed the lush green foliage that hugged the walls of the parsonage. It was covered in English primroses. He reached down, taking the small clippers he had brought with him. He gently snipped off handfuls of the brilliant garnet, cobalt blue, and pale yellow flowers, with their deeper yellow centers. He was gentle, examining each cluster carefully as he cut the first of several stems that were bending in the winter breeze. He did not want to harm a single one. Growing nearby, he eyed some delicate white blooms. He delighted in the deep gold stamen of each center, popping out like miniature bouquets. These would also grace his gift to Marcie.

Samuel walked to the stream, carrying his bouquet. Finding nothing he returned to the parsonage. He asked Chen if he could include some winter pansies in his gift of flowers. After receiving permission from the reverend, he returned to the garden and clipped some of the colorful pansies that were planted in clay pots that lined the pebbled path. His face lit up when he saw the different shades of purple, yellow, and blue, with their deep, dark velvety centers. Samuel took his index finger and stroked the smooth pedals.

When he returned to the parsonage, Samuel placed the short stems of the pansies in a paper cup and added water. He took a rubber band from the utility drawer and wrapped it around the long stems of his bouquet, adding tin foil to the bottom. He hoped Marcie would keep the cup with pansies on her nightstand.

Samuel knocked gently on Marcie's door. "Come in," Marcie beckoned. "Come closer, Samuel, please sit." She smiled as he handed her his gift of flowers.

"I picked these in the garden for you." Samuel was beaming. He excused himself and went back to the kitchen. He took the cup with pansies from the counter and returned to Marcie's room. He placed the cup on her nightstand. "How are you feeling? Are you very sick?" Samuel asked.

"First of all, thank you for the flowers, Samuel, they are beautiful, and the pansies are so colorful. I will think of you whenever I look at them."

Samuel was pleased he made Marcie smile. "I'm getting better each day," Marcie said. "Soon I will have my baby. When he or she is born, we can take walks down to the lake, and we can show the baby the wildlife that comes by."

"I would love to walk down with you and the baby. We can watch the geese fly over the water."

Samuel visited Marcie for about half an hour. "I would like to rest now," she said softly. Please come again soon. I enjoyed your visit, Samuel, and thank you again for the flowers. They are lovely."

~~~

The winter snow blanketed the countryside, and the canals nearly froze. Skiers showed up in droves. They avoided the expensive resorts in the mountains and chose to lodge in the foothills, taking advantage of whatever Camwood had to offer. Marcie was nearing the end of her pregnancy. Samuel stopped by from time to time to check up on her. Niki doted on her like a mother hen, and Chen became the strong mentor she needed.

Marcie's story of how she became pregnant had troubled Chen so much so that the day after Marcie walked into his church Chen went back on his promise to keep it to himself. He made an appointment with the chief of police, who was assigned to a different unit during Chen's junior detective days. He felt guilty and asked God to forgive him. However, if her story were true, Chen knew the boy who attacked Marcie needed to be held accountable for what he had done. He reasoned, the boy's parents would want to know they had a grandchild about to be born, and if they were responsible parents, they would want their son to own up to the crime of rape if he were to be found guilty.

~~~

The 7th precinct was located in the historical town of Camwood, west of the theatre district. Its old Edwardian architecture with its small cubicles left most of the staff disheartened. They longed for a modern building with open spaces.

Chief Darrell Dugan had taken charge of the police department not long after Chen resigned from the police force. The chief was a stocky man, about five foot eleven.

He was in his late forties. He shaved his reddish brown hair faithfully, rather than admit he was going bald. The color of his hair, or what was left of it, was evident in his eyebrows, his thin moustache, and his thick goatee which was dusted with gray. He never spoke of his family. He just showed up each day. Those under him didn't know if he was married, or ever had been, and he never spoke of having children, at least not to them. The officers under his authority never asked; they couldn't have cared less.

The chief ran his department like a general, spewing orders on the hour. He maintained a close relationship with the heads of the homicide division and the forensics department as well as other branches within his jurisdiction, and he got things done. There were few unsolved cases on his desk.

~~~

Chen had arrived at the Camwood Police Department on a Monday afternoon. Police Chief, Darrell Dugan, had not known Chen well. Darrell was promoted to the head of his department after Chen left law enforcement, but he had seen Chen from time to time. Darrell welcomed him and offered him a seat. The two men shook hands and Chen sat.

The building was cold and uninviting. *No changes here,* Chen thought. The cubicles that housed the staff didn't make them any warmer, and the daily complaints rolled off the chief's back.

"What brings you to our neck of the woods, Pastor?" Darrell asked.

"Chief, what I am about to divulge must be kept between us until you check it out. I don't want anyone to be falsely accused of such a heinous crime unless you are absolutely sure what I say is true."

"You have my word," Darrell responded.

Chen relayed how Marcie came to him and Niki. He described the details of Marcie's attack as it was told to him.

In time, she had revealed to him the name of the boy. Was it her way of wanting closure?

Darrell's face paled as he listened. "I know the family. They are well respected here in Camwood. In fact, they are big supporters of the police, not only here in town, in other counties as well. They contribute often."

Chen's countenance took on a look of defeat. Darrell leaned toward Chen. His eyes narrowed, and he raised his deep tone. "You can be sure we will get at the truth," he howled. "I don't care how much they are worth to our department. I will not let that sway me at all in their favor."

"I will need a DNA test to corroborate Marcie's account of what took place, Darrell requested. The family is well-to-do, and the boy's father is an assemblyman. He will have the best lawyers. Because the boy is a minor, we have to get parental consent to test him. I doubt they will cooperate. I can only hope he will confess to the attack. In either case, a DNA test will have to be performed once the baby is born if we are to find out who the father is."

The pastor extended his hand to Chief Dugan.

"I will contact the boy's parents and make an appointment to visit with them. If possible, I will try to question the boy." Darrell said. "I have a feeling the parents will not allow it. If what you say is true and the boy doesn't admit to the assault, we can expect a small war will take place in Camwood."

## CHAPTER TWENTY-ONE
### (The Misfortune 2002)

January showed no mercy. The temperature was below freezing, and the Camwood lakes were a sheet of thick glass. Samuel missed the weekends he had spent fishing. Marcie was about to give birth any day, and Chen and Niki were spending the cold days tending to the needs of their congregation. There were visits to the elderly and the sick, and food had to be delivered to the hungry. Marcie had taken a turn for the better, and her toxemia seemed to be under control.

~~~

Samuel asked Chen if he could visit Marcie on Saturday morning. Chen agreed. Samuel arrived early and knocked softly on Marcie's door.

Marcie was always happy to see Samuel. He became a younger brother to her; one she never had but wanted. She invited Samuel to come in. "What have you been up to," Marcie asked.

"Not much," Samuel replied. "Just hanging around in my spare time. How are you feeling? Will the baby come soon?"

"Yes, Samuel, very soon. Maybe this week, I'm not sure. When God wants him or her to make an entrance into this world, he or she will come. What are you planning to do this weekend?"

"Go down to the lake to watch the skaters."

"Please be careful, Samuel. Always tell your mother what your plans are. Let her know where and when you are going. Everything is frozen now, but we all need to be cautious. The sun can melt ice on the lake quickly, do you understand?" "Let us know also," she added. Samuel nodded. "Make sure you obey the rules," Marcie advised.

"Yes, I will tell my mother and Chen where I am." Samuel smiled and waved goodbye. He closed Marcie's door quietly and left the parsonage.

~~~

The weekend forecast was in the freeze zone. Samuel decided he would change into his heaviest jacket and take his dog, Archie, along. He would go down to the lake with Archie at his side.

Jeanette was in the kitchen, preparing a lunch for Samuel. She added utensils, napkins, and a thermos filled with hot chocolate to the lunch pail. "I don't think you should take Archie with you Son, it's too cold."

Samuel's lower lip curled, and his eyes remained focused on the green and beige tiles of the floor.

"Remember the safety measures you've been taught. Go, Samuel. Have fun!"

Samuel nodded and ran to the closet to grab his winter jacket. He thanked his mother and took the lunch container from her. He patted Archie on the head as he bolted out the door.

Like blankets of white ashes scattered across the roads, the winding country lanes were covered in a dusting of frost. The sun appeared from behind the clouds, and the blankets of frost slowly disappeared, revealing the dark, frozen earth beneath.

Samuel continued to walk toward the lake, carrying his lunch pail with him. He was grateful for the warmth the sun was providing, but as quickly as the sun had appeared it vanished behind the clouds that had now turned a slate gray.

Samuel didn't have skates. Jeanette tried skating lessons, but Samuel was never able to master the skill, so she ignited an interest in him to learn how to fish. The sport had become a blessing to both Jeanette and Samuel. But now it was winter. He would have to wait until spring.

Samuel enjoyed going down to the lake to watch the young folks gliding and twirling across the ice. He imagined himself skating with a friend, holding each other up, reaching the other side of the lake—and skating back. He would dream of competing in sports activities, like other young people, but he remained content to watch. He had attended ball games and soccer games with Chen, and they occasionally shot a few baskets at the high school court. Each time, he would pretend he made the winning score. Samuel was a dreamer!

The wind picked up as fresh snow spiraled from above. Samuel glanced heavenward and pulled his neck scarf up to protect his face. He had thoughts of returning home, but as he drew nearer to the lake, voices coming from the skating area beckoned him to stay.

The weather plummeted to thirty degrees. The lake had been sectioned off with signs when and where to skate and which areas to avoid. About sixteen teenagers were off to one side, laughing as they skated and fell.

The unrelenting wind blew away some of the white dustings left by the new fallen snow. It revealed dark patches of ice, resembling small black mirrors. There seemed to be a tug of war between the sun and the clouds.

By late afternoon, the sun had won, allowing fresh snow to glisten on the lake's surface. It resembled a scene from a Currier and Ives catalogue or a Norman Rockwell painting.

Underneath the frigid lake's surface, the temperature rose to about forty degrees. This higher temperature would allow the fish to survive the winter. It always did.

Samuel had eaten his lunch, and he continued to watch the young couples as they skated. For at least an hour, he sat on an old bench made of soft pinewood and metal. The bench had been donated by the Camwood Chamber of

Commerce. He often sat there. He was bundled up in his winter garb and could barely turn his head. He had forgotten to take his watch and sensed it was getting late. He decided to return home.

The teens started to disappear, two by two, until only Samuel was left. As he turned to leave, far out onto the lake he eyed a red and blue checkered scarf. Wondering who it belonged to, he thought he would bring it to the parsonage and place it in the lost and found closet in Chen's study. He hoped someone would search for it there.

The trees surrounding the lake were silent as Samuel approached its edge. He stepped forward and felt the hard surface. He continued to walk in small even steps until he was about five feet from the scarf.

Like a creaky door that needed oiling, he heard the crack of the ice beneath his feet. It took only seconds for Samuel to be swallowed under a frigid blanket of water and ice as fast as a vacuum sucks up the dirt, and there was no one around to witness the misfortune.

## CHAPTER TWENTY-TWO
### (The Lord's Whisper - January 2002)

Samuel was struggling for his life. One minute passed and then another. Under the icy water, he had an image of his mother Jeanette. He thought she was overprotective of him, but his winter jacket, made with a special foam lining, acted as a buoy, keeping his head above the water and close to the opening of the broken ice. He had given her a hard time when she purchased it. Now he was grateful.

Samuel was getting weaker. His arms and legs felt numb. He could not remember how long he was in the water, but hypothermia was beginning to set in. He kept trying to grab the jagged edges of the ice above his head. Several pieces broke off with his grasp. They fell into the frigid hole, which made the opening wider. Using the sun's rays as his guide, he bounced up and down so his head would be seen by anyone passing by. With what little energy he had left, his many cries for help went unheard.

~~~

The patrol car eased into its usual parking spot at the entrance to Camwood Lake. The cracking of ice could be heard under a dusting of fresh snow as the heavy snow tires rolled into place and came to a halt.

Officer John Riordan stopped by the lake often to check on the skaters. He zipped his jacket, and he adjusted his black felt hat and earmuffs. The wind picked up, and he tightened the red wool scarf around his neck. When his heavy boots hit the frozen ground, he heard the faint cries. His first instinct was to rush toward the lake. His boots burrowed into the pathway that hadn't yet been shoveled, leaving their impression behind and creating a path of their own. In his haste he took nothing with him.

Officer Riordan stared out onto the lake. He saw nothing was amiss. He turned and walked toward the recreation area, thinking the voice he heard may have been from another direction, perhaps some kids up to mischief near the picnic tables. Another cry for help rang out. It was coming from the far side of the lake beyond the trees. John turned and ran. "I'm coming, he shouted."

Repeatedly, the officer's voice called out. His words echoed silently in the formed vapor that vanished in the frigid winter air. In one split second he saw the top of a puffy black jacket with lime green stripes, those that were made to glow in the darkness for safety; then the stripes disappeared.

Officer Riordan was trained in different methods of ice rescue. There was no time to run back to the police car to grab a rope. He knew where and how to approach the frozen areas that would be safe. He was not heavyset, nor was he slim but of a medium build, and he knew as he came closer to the broken ice, he too would be in danger of falling into the abyss. He lay down on his left side and rolled toward the open hole. Once again, the figure in the black jacket and green stripes popped up, and he recognized it was Samuel.

"Hold on, Samuel, I'm here to help," Officer Riordan shouted. "Kick your legs until I can reach you."

When he reached the gaping hole, Samuel had exhausted the last bit of strength he had. "Kick, Samuel, kick," the officer continued to yell.

Samuel could feel his blood rushing through his body, but his energy was failing him and he was ready to succumb to his fate. With the final kick he mustered up, the officer took hold of the boy's right arm and locked it with his, keeping Samuel's face above the water. Officer Riordan pulled Samuel toward himself, comforting him and instructing him to stay calm. "Take deep, slow breaths,

Samuel, and listen to my instructions," John ordered. He held a tight grip and pulled the boy to safety.

"Now, Samuel, we are both going to roll toward the edge of the lake," the officer instructed.

"Yes," Samuel slurred, his body by now a victim to the stress.

"You will roll first, and I will be behind you to protect you. I promise you will not fall in as long as you are not walking with me on the ice. Now, you go first."

Samuel was always obedient when following someone's instructions in school or at church; it was not hard for him to listen and obey. He laid horizontally on the frozen ice's surface and slowly began to roll toward the trees in the distance. Officer Riordan followed, encouraging him with every roll.

When they reached the lake's edge, John picked up Samuel and carried him to the car. He placed an emergency call to the station and asked for an ambulance.
"They're on their way," the dispatcher replied.

The officer began to remove whatever wet clothing was possible. As hard as he tried, he could not get the zipper of Samuel's jacket to open. He grabbed a pair of scissors from his emergency kit and began to cut down the jacket's front. Once the jacket was removed, he was able to lift the boy's polar shirt above his head and pull it off. He removed his shoes and socks and wrapped him in several blankets. Samuel began to respond, mumbling a bit but making some sense. He was shivering, and the officer knew it was a way of compensating for the loss of body heat. He felt it was a good sign. Samuel's God given defenses were doing its job.

Officer Riordan had coffee left in his thermos and poured some into the cup. It was still warm. He asked Samuel to drink it. "You probably haven't had coffee before, and you may not like it, but it will help warm you up." Samuel obeyed, and he took sips of the warm liquid.

The ambulance pulled up next to the police car in a matter of minutes. Two EMT's rushed out and stood beside the car with a stretcher and blankets. Samuel was rushed to Charity Hospital with Officer Riordan following close behind.

The emergency team was waiting as the ambulance pulled up to the doors of the hospital's back entrance. Samuel stopped shivering, and his condition turned from mild to moderate hypothermia. They immediately started a re-warming process. His mother was notified. Jeanette called Chen, and he and Niki met her and Officer Riordan at the hospital within the hour.

The officer hung around for several hours. He was drenched. The staff offered him a gown, blankets, and a warm drink. He refused to leave Charity Hospital until they were notified that Samuel had responded to treatment.

No one knows how long Samuel was in the frozen lake. To this day, Officer John Riordan felt it was the Lord Who had whispered in his ear to check out Camwood Lake, an hour earlier.

## CHAPTER TWENTY-THREE
### (Welcome To the World - January 2002)

On Wednesday night, around ten p.m., Marcie began to experience mild pain. Chen and Niki had gone to bed early, expecting to make a few hospitality calls in the morning. Marcie would wait before waking up the couple. Her contractions were about half a minute long and not much under ten minutes apart. She had read enough to know she was in the early stages of labor.

Marcie's back ached, so she decided to take a shower and afterwards pack some things for her stay at Charity Hospital. The warm steam from the shower helped as it enveloped her body, and she felt comforted. She knew early labor could last for many hours and tried to go back to sleep. She was able to doze in intervals.

In between dozing, Marcie would stare at the ceiling, wondering what gender her baby would be and who it would look like. She didn't want a relationship with the boy responsible for her pregnancy, but she thought of his parents. *Would they want to know the baby? Would my own parents want to know him or her? Which family would it resemble the most?*

At eight a.m. the following morning, Marcie went into active labor. Niki had been up for over an hour, and breakfast was hot and on the table. She greeted Marcie. After one look, Niki hurried to the study to alert Chen. "We have to go. Marcie's in labor."

Chen jumped up, grabbed his car keys and ran toward the old willow to start the engine. The ladies followed. Niki carried Marcie's overnight bag, and both ladies hurried to the car.

~~~

The hospital staff greeted the trio and advised Chen and Niki to return home and wait. "Labor can go on for hours, better to go home and rest. We will contact you in time to return and be here for Marcie when she gives birth."

It was another four hours before Chen and Niki received a call from the hospital staff to return; Marcie was about to give birth.

The couple arrived in time. Donning masks and gowns they entered the delivery room. They found Marcie awake and grateful they would be there to witness the new life about to make an entrance into the world. Chen was beaming; *Another wonderful soul for God's kingdom!*

Grace Rose made her debut at exactly 1:45 p.m. on Thursday, January 31st, 2002. She was 6 lbs. 4 oz. She was small, like her mother, and her hair was light and full. Marcie held her daughter in her arms while the Youngs watched with joyful tears. They held hands and prayed that this new life would come to know and serve God.

## CHAPTER TWENTY-FOUR
### (Gathering Evidence - February 2002)

Since their last encounter at the police station, Chen had not contacted Chief Darrell Dugan. Chen knew there was a battle ahead. Marcie refused to press charges, and Chen remained in limbo. He reasoned if their son was indeed the father of Grace Rose, the parents of the boy who attacked Marcie should know of the attack and that they had a grandchild.

Chen approached the door of the sheriff's office and knocked. Through the frosted glass pane, Darrell recognized the image was Chen's. "Come in," he said warmly. He stood and smiled, offering his hand. Darrell motioned for Chen to take a seat across from him.

Chen was troubled, and Darrell picked up on it. "You look worried," Darrell said.

"I'm deeply concerned. I'm at a loss."

"I don't blame you. I get it!"

"Marcie gave birth yesterday to a beautiful baby girl, Grace Rose. Marcie's alone in the world, and we are here for her. She is welcome to stay with us as long as she needs to. I was wondering if you followed up on the parents of the teen? I think they would want to know they had a grandchild, that is, if the boy *is* the father. I also hope they would want their son to be accountable, if he is guilty."

Darrell took a few seconds before he spoke. He pressed on the intercom button and directed his secretary to hold all calls. He filled Chen in on what took place after his visit to their home. "I went to see the boy's parents. I told them Marcie's account of what happened at the school. They did not take it well and accused me of targeting their son.

They said it was political because the father was running for re-election in the spring—this time for governor. I told them I had no political agenda, and I was only trying to get to the bottom of things. I explained Marcie was living with you and your wife at the parsonage. I asked if they would agree to a DNA test for their son. They refused. I didn't get a chance to question the boy alone, but he was present when I visited his parents. Of course, he denied having anything to do with her."

Chen felt defeated. He was about to thank Darrell and leave. Darrell stopped him.

"Wait, I'm not through. It's too late to search for DNA samples in the janitors' closet where the assault took place. The custodians complained, and they were given a bigger space. The closet where the crime took place has been thoroughly cleaned and painted. They added extra shelves, and the space is now being used to store classroom materials. We checked."

Chen stood and walked toward the door. The chief patted his shoulder. "Look, if we can get a sample from him, we can test it against the baby's DNA and see if we get a match. That won't be hard. He eats in the lunchroom every day at school, I'm sure. I could have one of my officers wait around and grab a utensil or cup he used—even a napkin."

"If it's a positive match, how do you deal with the parents?"

"Leave that to me. They will have to consent to it first and sign a release. I'll hold on to the sample and hope they agree. I've seen this before. Sooner or later, they will want to know the truth."

Chen thanked the Chief and left with the hope Marcie would have some closure.

## CHAPTER TWENTY-FIVE
### (Mission Accomplished - February 2002)

The day was warmer than usual. The beautiful white landscape of Camwood had turned to gray slush, matching the overcast sky. Hank Merrill had been under Chief Darrell Dugan's supervision for the past year and was considered a rookie cop by his fellow officers. He was out on duty, cruising the streets and searching for stranded cars. The morning rush was in full gear and accident reports were being called into 911, from fender benders to serious collisions. The collisions took priority.

By late morning, things had quieted down. The chief picked up the receiver. "Radio Merrill and ask him to return to the station," he requested of dispatch.

Fifteen minutes passed. Hank Merrill bolted through the office door. "Chief, are you looking for me?"

"Yes Merrill, I have a new assignment for you. It'll put another experience under your belt. I want you to go to Camwood High School. Ask the office secretary what time the senior class has lunch. When you find out, I want you to return at that exact time. Go directly to the lunch room. Ask one of the students to point out the person I want you to observe. If you are questioned by anyone, say you are on your break."

Darrell identified the teenager to Hank, giving him a name and complete description of the boy. "We need a sample from him. It can be anything he ate or drank from. If he throws his can of soda into the trash, grab it before anyone else goes near it. I'll have it tested. It might be useful one day."

"I'm on my way, Chief."

~~~

Hank Merrill was tall and slim, with curly blond hair, and deep set, dark blue eyes. He had graduated from the Police Academy after taking criminal justice classes in college. He grew up in Camwood and most people in town knew him. He was in his late twenties, unmarried, and the local girls couldn't have cared less.

Hank lived far from the town and the canals that twisted like hawser ropes connected to its moorings. He lived with his parents, on the north side, where the streams emptied into the nearby rivers and lakes. He wanted to save the world as most young folk do, so he chose a career in law enforcement.

~~~

Hank arrived at the school at eleven o'clock. He went directly to the high school office to inquire when the lunch break would be for the senior class.

"Twelve-fifteen," the secretary exclaimed.

"Do you mind if I hang around and observe the kids?"

The school secretary, Julie, knew Hank since he had attended middle school. She didn't question him further. "Sure, go ahead, enjoy yourself. I'm busy Hank so go about your business and have a nice day." Julie smiled.

Hank was glad that was over. He left the school building and returned to his vehicle. He sat there for an hour, listening to the police radio. At noon, he returned to the school. He walked to the cafeteria and stood against the wall to the right of the entrance doors. He waited.

The bell rang out, and a storm of hungry students bolted down the hall and into the lunchroom. Hank eyed a girl who was taking her time. She was wearing black jeans with a yellow wool sweater, and she was chewing gum. He stopped her before she could enter the lunchroom. "Hello,

I'm Officer Hank." She looked at him bewildered. He gave her a description of the boy and asked if she knew him.

"Oh yes, there he is," she answered, between snaps of gum. "He's in the red shirt." She pointed. Her long blond ponytail swayed as she walked away from the officer and scurried into the cafeteria.

The officer remained in the doorway. At least he had a suspect. He watched the teenager, as he ate his lunch and drank a citrus drink from a can. After finishing his meal, the boy rose and headed toward the trash can that was situated next to the exit door.

Officer Hank moved to the exit side. He watched as the boy emptied the contents of his tray into the trash. The boy placed the empty tray on a stand with the other used trays and strolled down the hallway, making a right turn into the corridor that led to his classroom. He was still holding the can of juice, taking sips as he walked. Hank walked faster and passed him.

The boy's teacher was standing at the classroom door, waiting to receive her class. Hank approached her, smiling. He didn't want to go into the classroom and make a scene. He was polite and tried not to look apprehensive, but his countenance said the opposite. The teacher recognized him.

"How are you Hank, what brings you to our school today?" Karen Post asked.

Hank smoothed his hair and cleared his throat. "Just taking a break. I thought I'd come in and say hello to some of my old friends. How have you been?" he asked, avoiding her eyes.

"Things are good," she answered, half-heartedly.

Eyeing the teen about to approach the classroom door, the officer jumped at his chance. "Are the students allowed to bring food into class after the bell rings?"

"No, as a matter of fact."

"Then I'll do my good deed for the day." Hank took the can out of the boy's hand. Actually, he grabbed it, turned and walked briskly away, not giving Karen the opportunity to take the can away from the boy herself.

Hank looked over his shoulder and smiled. "Have a good day," he said, as he strutted down the hall. Karen looked at him oddly, shrugged her shoulders and walked into the classroom. Hank exited the school and disappeared into the parking area.

There was a time Hank had taken a liking to Karen. He was shy and a few invitations short of asking her out. He sensed she would not have been interested in him, and his sense was correct. Her cool demeanor at the school confirmed it.

When Hank reached the police car, he opened the glove compartment and took out a brown paper bag. He carefully placed the juice can in the bag. He avoided the areas the boy used to drink from and tied it closed. Mission accomplished!

Was Chief Darrell Dugan doing the right thing obtaining a sample for DNA, without getting permission from the boy's parents? Hank wondered.

## CHAPTER TWENTY-SIX
(Kowloon -The Sketches)

In 1989, the Tiananmen Square riots had erupted. Living under communist rule, the young students of Beijing cried out for democracy. They wanted free speech and free press. There were hunger strikes and sit-ins. The military was called in and hundreds, maybe even thousands, no one knows for sure, were slaughtered mercilessly. A number of those who survived the massacre migrated to Hong Kong. The Chinese government was able to stop others, but some made it through to the island. China protested the migrations, and the Hong Kong politicians finally gave in.

The protests became a red flag to the Young family, who had once felt safe on the island. How long would it take for Chinese authoritarian rule to take over the whole of Hong Kong? It gave Li and Hua the incentive to save every penny to make their journey to the West.

During this time, Chen had been in the Untied States for five years. He had completed his last year of college and was taking post graduate classes in Criminal Justice. He planned to attend the Police Academy after he completed his courses. He and his parents corresponded often, but he didn't have the money to send for them. He avoided the issue in his letters, and Li and Hua understood. Their plan was to save the money themselves and one day surprise their son.

~~~

Many seasons passed, and Li Young continued to work at the Kowloon factory. He was a master at his trade. In his spare time, he would sketch designs of men's apparel and keep them in a brown leather satchel which he took to work with him. Some designs were of dress shirts and some were of trousers and jackets. He never thought of it as a talent, he just wanted to pass the time.

~~~

Li had finished his shift and left for the day. He hurried to the pier to catch an earlier ferry to Hong Kong Island. In his haste he left his satchel next to a window that was located near his workstation.

Manager Wang Wei was doing a last minute check of his department before the arrival of the evening shift. He passed the window, and his eyes were drawn to the leather briefcase on the floor. Wondering who it belonged to, he took it to his office and placed it in the closet opposite his desk. He stood for a moment trying to decide if he should open it. The temptation to take a look inside won over the respect of someone's privacy.

Wang had seen Li with a brown satchel before. He surmised it was Li's. Wang lifted it and brought it to his desk. He unleashed the straps and pressed the brass latch, hoping it was not locked. The top flap loosened and Wang opened it. It contained a manila folder that was filled with papers. Wang took out the folder and went through its contents. His eyebrows arched and his eyes widened. What he discovered was a treasure trove of fashion; designs created by a master artist.

Wang knew his trade. Before coming into the management position at the Kowloon factory, he had designed a few pieces that were bought by the Kwon family. They produced the clothing under their own label, and he was paid a high price for the sketches. As Wang got older, he showed no interest in creating anything new, but he knew talent and creativity when he saw it. He wanted Li Young to succeed.

Wang put the contents of the satchel back as he had found it. His problem would be admitting to Li that he had invaded his privacy, yet he wanted him to be acknowledged for his talent. He felt he owed him that much.

~~~

It wasn't until Li Young was on the ferry ride to Hong Kong that he discovered he had forgotten his designs. His first response was panic. Every design he ever created was in his folder. He hoped it would still be there when he returned in the morning.

Hua would not be returning to work until Monday evening, so she was not an option to rescue him. Li would have to try and contact Manager Wang Wei, but how? A phone was a luxury they could not afford.

Li disembarked the ferry, hoping to meet someone on the pier who worked the late shift. He waited until it was about to cross the bay for a return trip to Kowloon. Not recognizing anyone boarding who worked at the factory, he walked to the train station and headed for home. By the time he reached his train stop, it began to pour. He had forgotten to take an umbrella that morning, so he ran the rest of the way home.

Hua was in the kitchen area preparing a hot meal. Li was drenched. Hua offered him a towel and told him to change while she continued to prepare dinner.

Because of the weather they decided to spend the rest of the evening indoors. Li remained quiet; he did not want to burden Hua with another problem.

"Why don't you work on your designs," Hua suggested. "I'll read."

"I'm tired, the shift seemed longer than usual. I'm going to rest."

"Are you feeling all right?"

"Yes, I want to rest." No other words were spoken.

Li had battled with insecurities for many years. He knew Hua was stronger than he was, and she could figure things out more easily. She was comfortable around others she knew, and she had no problem relating to strangers. Li was an introvert. He would be the first to leave a room filled with people or not show up at all. He wanted to live his life with two other people, his wife and his son. His way of dealing with a certain problem was to avoid the issue with his daydreaming.

The last thing Li wanted this night was for Hua to find out he had lost his sketches. It would only make him look weaker. He didn't want her to preach to him about being responsible. The fact was, she wouldn't have.

~~~

The following morning brought scattered showers. Li left earlier than usual and arrived at the ferry with extra time to spare. His mood was as foreboding as the darkened sky. Lightening sliced through the clouds like a steel blade, and the rain erupted with a vengeance. He had remembered to take his umbrella and remained on the outer deck. He looked for anyone he knew who was on the same shift. He would ask if they had seen his leather satchel upon leaving the day before.

The waters started to stir, and the ferry jostled against the waves like two wrestlers during a match. Visibility was dense. Fog horns were blasting, as captains tried to avoid crashing into each other. Li felt nauseous. He had taken the ferry a thousand times before; he had never gotten seasick. Today was an exception. He thought of getting on the next ferry back to the island when the boat reached Kowloon. He was succumbing to the deep pit of depression.

~~~

Manager Wang Wei was in his office. Every few minutes he would peek out the window into the massive sewing room and look for Li Young's arrival. He was grinning from ear to ear.

Li Young arrived at the factory before the start of his shift and walked to his workstation. He looked at the window where he had left his satchel. He saw nothing. He placed his umbrella in a receptacle nearby and hung his wet jacket on the back of his chair, hoping it would dry before the return trip home. He walked to Wang's office and knocked on the door. Wang had seen him coming and hurried to his desk. "Come in." he said. He was beaming.

"Manager Wei, I'm sorry to disturb you. I am not feeling well and request that I can return home to rest."

"Mr. Young, please sit. I will make you some hot tea. Maybe it will help." Wang walked over to the double burner that was resting on a table beneath the window. "Milk tea will be too heavy for you. I will serve you fresh ginger tea, it will be good for your stomach."

Li became uncomfortable. "Manager Wei, I have to get back to my station. I wanted to ask you…"

"You cannot go until you've had your tea," Wang interrupted.

Wang Wei took some fresh ginger root and finely grated it into a kettle. He added water and placed the kettle on the burner to boil. Within several minutes, the pent-up steam began to whistle. It howled through the kettle like a wounded animal, its shrill making Li's headache worse. "It will take a few minutes to settle, and you can have your tea," Wang said. Buying himself extra time, he allowed the ginger to steep in the kettle a bit longer.

Wang took a ceramic cup from the shelf behind his desk and added two lemon slices to the bottom. He lifted the kettle and strained the hot liquid into the large cup. He placed the cup before Li.

Li didn't want to argue with his superior. He sat quietly for a few moments and stared into the cup. The tea's pale golden color stared back at him. For a second, he closed his eyes and thought of the many cups of tea his grandmother had made for him growing up in Beijing. He took a few sips and cleared his throat. "Manager Wei, I left a leather satchel when my shift ended yesterday. It was brown. It was near my desk under the window. Did anyone return it to you?"

Wang Wei walked to the closet. He took the satchel lying on the closet floor and handed it to Li. For a moment, Li was unable to speak. His eyes became moist. He stood and made short bows before Wang. With each bow Li said, "Thank you, kind sir."

"Mr. Young, I beg you to stay a few more moments. Finish your tea, then I will give you leave to go home and rest."

Li was puzzled, but he obeyed. To be polite, he tried taking sips of tea from the cup.

Less than a minute passed. There was a knock on the door. Li felt he was going to collapse. His head throbbed and his body trembled.

Wang Wei ordered the visitor to enter. The man was of medium height, and his hair the color of and salt and pepper. He was dressed in Western clothing. His gray suit and gray on gray tie were made of the finest silk. He wore black shoes made of Italian leather and a Panerai designer watch on his right wrist. He spoke English. His accent was from the Lombardy region of Italy. He bowed slightly and greeted the two men. Manager Wang Wei, who spoke both English and Cantonese, acted as translator.

"Mr. Li Young, I would like you to meet Mr. Vincenzo Moncini. He is visiting us from Milan, Italy. He's here on business. I took the liberty of showing him the contents of your leather satchel." Wang made no apology for the snooping. In fact, he was giddy.

"Mr. Moncini is a renowned designer. I will let him speak now." Wang said.

Li took notice of the stranger's olive complexion, oval face, and sharp, straight nose. *His features would stand out in any crowd,* Li imagined.

Vincenzo Moncini extended his hand to Li Young. Li rose from his chair and returned the bow. They shook hands. "I'm delighted to make your acquaintance," Li said. His tone was timid.

"Mr. Young, I've had the liberty of seeing your designs. They are the work of a true artist. If you turn over your designs to our label, Moncini Originals of Milan, I will make you a generous offer, one you cannot refuse. You will have enough to live in comfort for the rest of your life."

Li was speechless. He had never thought of himself as an artist; a designer that had a future. His sketches were his own, to create and look at from time to time, but never this!

Vincenzo Moncini was grinning. "What do you say Mr. Young? Can you work with us? Of course, any new designs you come up with..." he paused, "you will be handsomely paid." A smile radiated across his face. "We can offer you a generous deal for *all* of your talent."

Li's vision of leaving Hong Kong and being with his son was enough to make the tears he was holding back fall freely. He had no shame.

"Will you shake on it, Mr. Young?"

Li didn't hesitate long. "Yes," he said with grateful enthusiasm, "Yes."

## CHAPTER TWENY-SEVEN
### (A Can of Juice - February 2002)

Holding a brown paper bag containing an empty can of citrus drink, Officer Hank Merrill bolted into Chief Darrell Dugan's office. "Here you go, Chief, I think this is what you are looking for."

Chief Dugan banged the phone down. "This call can wait. Well done, Hank! I'll take care of the rest. You can go back to the streets now." Officer Hank Merrill left the room and headed out the door to cruise his assigned area.

Chief Dugan picked up the phone and placed a call to Eric Austice, head of the forensic imaging lab uptown. "I have something for you Eric. I'm sending a messenger over this afternoon. I need a DNA on a can of juice. One of my men picked it up today. I'll arrange for a blood sample to be sent. I need a match before I can take this case further."

"Send it over, we'll wait for the sample. As soon as we get the results, we'll notify you."

~~~

Eric Austice was the best in the business. He was a master at his craft, earning his degree in Criminalistics from Syracuse University in upstate New York; one of the best learning institutions for forensic science. In his thirty-five years of analyzing evidence from thousands of crime scenes, his findings had helped law enforcement in the prosecution of the guilty and the redemption of those falsely accused.

Darrell had complete trust in Eric. He trusted Eric's findings would be precise. Maybe Marcie will get some closure.

~~~

Chief Darrell Dugan had a few folders of unresolved cases on his desk. He had planned to tackle one of them in the afternoon. Teen robberies were not uncommon. Fender benders and traffic violations could be handled by his staff. Instead, he locked up his files and headed for the parking lot.

It took about fifteen minutes before the chief entered the parsonage's driveway. He noticed Chen's car parked under the old willow. He was hoping to find Marcie at home. He wanted everyone present when he made his request. Chen was in his study catching up on some prayer requests. Chief Dugan's passion to help Marcie was evident in his forceful knock on the door.

No one responded. Darrell pushed the door open and walked in. "Anybody home?" he yelled.

"I am," Chen yelled back. "Come on in, I could use a break about now."

Chen approached the door and greeted the chief. He called Niki and asked her to bring a pot of hot coffee and a few cookies.

The two men entered the study. Darrell pulled up a chair near Chen's desk and sat. "I have some good news," he exclaimed.

Chen leaned closer. "What's up?"

"I've obtained a sample for DNA testing. If it matches Grace Rose's sample, we will have our attacker."

Chen stood and shook the officer's hand. "I can't thank you enough, Chief Dugan." He asked the chief to wait. In a matter of minutes Niki showed up with a tray of cookies, two cups of steaming coffee, a pitcher of milk and some sugar packets. Chen asked if she would bring Marcie to the study.

Niki returned with Marcie, who was holding Grace Rose. Marcie was visibly shaken. The chief spoke; his tone was soft. "Marcie, we need your permission to obtain a blood sample from Grace Rose, if that's okay with you?" His brow wrinkled. "We can't proceed without it."

Chen and Niki remained quiet. They wanted Marcie to make the decision for herself.

"You are in control of the situation, Marcie." Chief Dugan explained. "We understand if you don't want to proceed. However, if you don't go ahead with the test, you will never have closure. Am I making myself clear? This is an important decision."

Marcie shifted in her chair. She looked over at the door. She wanted to run. She didn't. She tried to compose herself and answered the chief of police. "I told you before— all of you, I don't want proof." She eyed each one as she spoke, "I don't want anything to do with him!"

Chief Dugan took her by the hands. "Marcie, listen closely. One day, in the future, you may need use of the father's name. In fact, he knows about Grace Rose, and when he becomes man enough he may want to have a relationship with her. That will be up to the courts.

"You can't forget your daughter has grandparents, and one day they may also want to know her. You may not want to deny either of them the chance to have a relationship with your daughter. If you change your mind, if this ever goes to trial, the father of Grace Rose may go to jail. He has to account for what he has done. I'm only asking you to consider these things. I understand if you won't. I will stop by tomorrow and hope you can give me your consent to continue the investigation."

Chief Dugan said his goodbyes in the hallway and saw himself out. On the drive back to the station he prayed. He was not a religious man. He didn't pray often, but he was involved enough in the case to whisper a prayer. He prayed Marcie would see the big picture.

## CHAPTER TWENTY-EIGHT
### (An Answered Question 2002)

February had kept its promise. The radio announcer confirmed it and predicted a cold front. He advised his listeners to bundle up. Chief Darrell Dugan jumped into the shower. By 7:30 a.m., he was dressed and sitting at the kitchen table. He had set the timer the night before so his coffee would brew itself in the morning. He ate a quick breakfast of cereal and toast, filled his thermos with the hot brew and bolted out the door.

Darrell decided he would stop at the parsonage, on his way to the Camwood Police Station. He wanted to see if Marcie had made up her mind about the DNA test. When Darrell arrived he found Marcie in the kitchen. She was preparing a hot breakfast for the Youngs. He asked if she would mind if he stayed.

"Of course, you can stay," she responded.

"Have you put any thought into what I asked you yesterday?"

"I have Chief. I prayed about it. I know I am young. Maybe when I'm older I will have regrets, but the one regret I will *never* have," she paused, "is that I gave birth to Grace Rose."

"What have you decided?"

"I have decided to go ahead with the DNA test. You can speak to Grace's doctor and have him send someone here. I will allow a technician to draw Grace's blood, but I want it to be done at the parsonage."

The chief was relieved. "I'll get on it right away," he said. "Give my regards to the Youngs." He thanked Marcie and left for the station house.

Darrell didn't wait for the elevator. As soon as he reached the station house, he ran up the flight of stairs two at a time. He went to his office and picked up the receiver. He dialed the number to Charity Hospital and asked for Doctor Neil Gorden.

The doctor was paged and called to the nurses' station. He had been making his rounds in the nursery and pediatric intensive care units. He picked up the phone and heard the chief on the other end.

"I'm sorry to bother you Doc, but I have an urgent request."

"No problem Chief Dugan. I'm about finished with my rounds. What can I do for you?"

"My request is that you arrange a DNA sample to be taken from Grace Rose. We've obtained a sample we can compare it with. Marcie has agreed to the test. Would this be possible?"

"Marcie is still a minor. I am obligated to ask her parents regarding the DNA test for their daughter's child."

"The parents want nothing to do with her."

"Let me get back to you. I will speak to my lawyer and find out what her rights are. I'll be in touch."

"Don't let it be too long, okay."

"I hear you."

~~~

It took a few days for the doctor to get back to Chief Dugan. "I'm sorry it took so long. My lawyer was out of town," Doctor Gorden apologized. "In this state if the mother of the child is a minor, she must have parental consent or a legal guardian's permission."

Chief Dugan collapsed in his chair. He felt defeated. "This does change things. We will need to speak to Marcie's parents. If they refuse, what then?"

The doctor was sympathetic. "If you want my advice, I believe you have two choices. You can befriend the parents and ask for their consent, or you can have the Youngs request legal guardianship in a court of law. That also involves parental consent. After all, she's been living with the Youngs for a while. It's up to you. This may take months."

Chief Dugan thanked the doctor. He decided to pay another visit to the parsonage on the weekend. He would present the options to the family then.

## CHAPTER TWENTY-NINE
### (A Big Decision - February 2002)

Several weeks had passed since Samuel's near drowning, and he was back to being Samuel. His ordeal set him behind a bit in school, but with the help of his mother, Jeanette, he was able to catch up.

Grace Rose was growing fast. All her needs were being met by the Youngs. The newborn was beginning to recognize her mother's scent, and Niki thought she even recognized her. She would smile when Niki walked into the room.

Marcie was now seventeen. She looked forward to the day when she would turn eighteen and be able to make her own decisions. She remained grateful for the care and kindness the Youngs showed her.

Samuel visited Marcie and Grace Rose often. Marcie referred to him as Uncle Samuel. He lit up each time she said it.

Nothing was ever mentioned of the baby's father. The grandparents wanted nothing to do with Grace Rose, and Marcie was resigned to it.

~~~

Chen received the call in the late afternoon on the following weekend. It was Saturday, the day he was to check the heating system in the sanctuary and make sure the sound system was working. After finishing, he returned to his study to go over his sermon. The call was from Darrell Dugan.

"Can I stop by? "I have some information for you," Chief Dugan added.

"I'm here Chief, please do."

It took twenty minutes for Darrell to arrive. Chen greeted the chief. "It's important that your wife hear what I have to say," Darrell said.

Niki came as soon as she was called. She greeted the chief of police. The couple invited Darrell to sit. "I hear you have some news for us," she said. She tilted her head to the side and waited.

"You both have taken full responsibility for Marcie and Grace Rose for some time now. You may want to think about filing for legal guardianship of Marcie. That will require parental consent. You can make the decisions her parents would have made, if she had not been estranged from them. I wanted to say this to you in private. I don't know your thoughts, but it's something to think about. The only alternative is to go to the parents and ask them to reconcile with her, so they can help with her medical and financial decisions."

Chen and Niki thanked Chief Dugan. After he left, they sat for a time and stared at each other. They both had the same thoughts. Chen broke the silence. "Should we go to her parents and ask them to take control of Marcie's life?" He paused. "If they refuse, should we offer to take on the responsibility of becoming Marcie's legal guardians and help to raise Grace Rose?" The couple discussed their options, and they prayed.

They didn't need to pray about it long. They looked at each other and smiled. They both agreed they wanted to have Marcie live with them indefinitely, but they also knew they would have to rescind if her parents had a change of heart.

"We will go see them tomorrow." Chen said. "We need an answer."

## CHAPTER THIRTY
### (A Dreaded Visit - February 2002)

The entrance to the development was gated. There was a guard at his post, sitting in a small booth reading a book. He had a radio beside him blasting reggae music. "How can he concentrate and read at the same time?" Niki was amazed. Chen noticed her expression. He laughed.

The booth was enclosed with a door and a window where the guard could speak to visitors. The tan Toyota pulled up to the window.

"Hello," the tall, dark man bellowed. His face was chiseled, with a square jaw and prominent chin. His accent was West Indian. He was deep toned and talked slowly, as if he were teaching the couple and not asking. "Who are you here to see today?" He smiled, exposing his white teeth.

"We called earlier. The party is expecting us. We are here to visit the Evanses."

The guard picked up the phone and made a call. He waved Chen and Niki on. "Enjoy your visit." He closed the window, the reggae music vanishing into the wind like puffs of smoke.

Hearing the last words of the song, the couple looked at each other and smiled. "You have to admit," Niki said, "it's good advice. It's what the Lord would want us to do, not worry. Didn't Jesus tell us that?"

"He did," Chen replied. "The outcome is in His hands."

As their car pulled up, Mr. and Mrs. Evans could be seen standing at the front door, a look of bewilderment on their faces. Chen did not tell them why he requested to see them. He mentioned he was a local pastor, and they agreed to the meeting. Maybe Phillip Evans thought it would help his campaign, if he should run for assemblyman. Chen was grateful. His introduction paved the way for dialog, and not the hang up call he was expecting.

The Evanses welcomed the young couple into their home and showed them into the living area.

"Please sit, Pastor," Phillip Evans said. His wife excused herself and stepped into the adjacent kitchen.

Marsha Evans was short in height, about five feet, with a dyed blond pageboy that stopped at her earlobes. She wore two large gold-plated circles, one attached to each lobe. She was of medium size, with piercing dark blue eyes and dark circles beneath, revealing she hadn't been getting much sleep. She wore a type of house dress, blue and green print with ties to the back. Her white house slippers were trimmed with imitation fur.

Chen took her apparel as a sign that she didn't think much of their visit. Marsha returned in a few minutes with hot tea and Ladyfingers.

"What brings you here, Pastor. Is this a courtesy visit?" Marsha Evans asked. She poured the tea and handed Chen the cup. "Please help yourself to milk and sugar, if you want."

"Thank you. Black tea is fine." Chen took the cup from Marsha and declined the Ladyfinger. Niki declined both. "I'm here to speak to you about your daughter, who is a congregant at our church." Chen lowered his head.

Marsha gasped and grabbed her husband's arm. Phillip was stony-eyed. "What has she been telling you about us, to bring you here for a meeting? She was …"

"Nothing really, Mr. Evans," Niki interrupted. "Marcie doesn't know we are here, so please don't fault her." Niki spoke softly, yet she showed no weakness in her tone.

"Your daughter was distraught, when she first came to our church. That was in June of last year. She told us she was two months pregnant. She also told us she was raped at school by a teenager." Chen said.

"Marcie told us the same thing, Pastor, and neither one of us believed her. She has always done what she wanted. We didn't seem to have control over her," Marcie's father said.

Chen leaned forward. "Mr. Evans, your daughter has given birth to a beautiful baby girl, Grace Rose. She was born this past January. Both Marcie and Grace Rose are living with us. When she first joined our church, she told us she was living in a shelter. Since that time, we have taken her in. We have grown to love both Marcie and Grace Rose, and we are providing for her. We want you to know if you are not willing to take her into your care, we are willing and able to do it."

Marsha's eyes became moist. She glanced at her husband. She didn't respond to Chen's suggestion. Phillip Evans did. "I believe my daughter is in a hole she dug for herself. I do not believe the rape story. Not one bit!" His face reddened as he raised his voice and backed away.

"Mr. Evans, may I interject?" Niki asked.

"Go ahead."

"Mr. Evans, the boy involved in the attack on your daughter is from a prominent family here in Camwood. I have been told the father, who is a political figure, is a very good friend of yours. Could this be why you refused to cooperate with Chief Dugan when he called on you? Is it also true you have political aspirations of your own and you are afraid a scandal involving you and the boy's father will upset your future plans? Please be forthright with us."

Phillip Evans remained quiet. He sat and lowered his head. He rested both hands on his temples.

For the first time since he arrived, Chen felt what the man was about to say would be the truth.

"I didn't believe my daughter, yes," Phillip Evans answered, "and what you say, Mrs. Young, is true." He glanced at Niki. "I am friends with the family involved, and I know the boy. I trusted him over my daughter. I put the thought of him raping her out of my mind." He paused for nearly a minute. The Youngs remained quiet. "Maybe I was in denial." "Maybe I still am," he added.

"If you believe what I am telling you now, or even if you don't, Chief Dugan would like to arrange for a DNA test. Will you be willing to accept the results?" Chen paused.

"Yes, I couldn't deny that."

"Mr. Evans, you, as her parent, would have to agree to the test. If you are not willing, my wife and I are willing to petition for legal guardianship of Marcie and Grace Rose. We would need your consent to do this. It would have to be legalized in court." Chen glanced at Marsha Evans. "This includes you also," he said.

"Can we get back to you on that? I can't give you an answer right now." Phillip Evans glanced at his wife, hoping for a reaction, but she showed no emotion. She did not respond to Chen's suggestion.

Chen and Niki sensed that Marcie's father may be having second thoughts. All four spoke a few minutes longer. They shook hands and parted.

The Youngs gave a wave to the guard who was bouncing his head and drumming his fingers to the music. They exited the gate and turned left onto the main road.

"How did they even have to think it over?" Niki's eyes were red. She took out her handkerchief and wiped her nose. "It's a no brainer, isn't it?"

"You'd be surprised. They are not the first, and they won't be the last."

"I hope we can get full guardianship," Niki cried. "Chen, why didn't they ask about the baby? They didn't show emotion, or curiosity. Don't they want to see her and know what she looks like? Who does she resemble? How much has she grown?"

"God's timing is perfect, Nik. He's in control, you know that! We will keep praying." Chen smiled and quoted the scripture verse in the book of Isaiah, 'In a favorable time I have answered you.'"

Chen checked his mirrors and entered the service road that led to the highway. "They may come around," he said. "We will wait a week. If they don't contact us, we will have the chief pay them another visit. We need the test done as soon as possible."

## CHAPTER THIRTY-ONE
### (A Return Visit - February 2002)

Six days had gone by. Chen and Niki had not heard from Marcie's parents, nor from Chief Dugan. They wondered if the DNA problem would be resolved. "I'm waiting one more day. If we don't hear from anyone, I'm going back. No use calling Phillip Evans, it will give him a chance to hang up, if he chooses to," Chen said.

"I can only think of one thing," Niki responded. "They are tied up politically with the boy's family. I heard a rumor in town that if the boy's father wins the election he will appoint Phillip Evans to a position on one of his committees. I also heard Phillip Evans will run for assemblyman to fill the vacancy left by the boy's father, if he should step down to finish his campaign. I have a feeling Marcie's father will choose that assignment. He will be getting the opportunity to join government politics, and that's probably what he wanted in the first place. A scandal will ruin his chances. You go see him, Chen." Niki insisted.

~~~

The drive to the Evanses' home was stressful for Chen. He mulled a thousand scenarios in his mind of what could take place. He was going unannounced. He didn't want to give Marcie's father the chance to refuse his visit.

Chen pulled off the parkway and made a right turn into the gated community. The West Indian man, from Jamaica, was seated at his station, the small booth blasting his country's music with a vengeance. He noticed the tan

Toyota and beckoned Chen to approach. He remembered the car. "How are you doing today, Man?" he asked.

"I'm doing fine. May I proceed?"

"Are your people expecting you?" His wide smile exposing his white teeth.

"I've been here before, don't you remember?" Chen asked. He said a silent prayer he would not be turned away.

"Hold on, while I call. What was the family's name again?" The guard reached for the phone.

"I see you have your country's music on. It sounds good. You might want to tone it down a bit."

"Oh yes, I can listen and read my book at the same time. I know all the words to all the songs."

"Listen, can you let me pass? I'm a bit late. I want to surprise the family before they leave. We all have plans." Chen was polite.

The phone rang. The guard turned his head for a moment, but not before he noticed Chen glancing at his watch. As the sentinel answered the call, he simultaneously lifted the gate and let the pastor through. He waved Chen on and delved deep into a conversation.

"Thank You, Lord," Chen whispered. He turned onto the street where he had been before and pulled the car in front of the Evanses' home, hoping they had not heard the car approaching. He walked up the drive and stood before the front door. There were two windows with small vertical panes, flanking the main entrance door. He could see Mr. and Mrs. Evans walking about the house so he knew they were home. He whispered another prayer and leaned hard on the bell.

Phillip Evans came to the door and opened it. His wife was standing behind him. When he discovered his visitor was Chen Young his look changed to one of astonishment. He almost closed the door in his face, a scenario Chen had envisioned on his way over.

Mr. Evans jerked his head back and gasped. His

demeanor was the opposite of when he greeted Chen a week earlier.

"What are you doing here, Mr. Young?" He avoided the title of Reverend.

"May I come in, it won't take long. Forgive me for showing up like this, but time is of the essence."

Phillip Evans reluctantly invited Chen into the living room. Chen sat, and Mr. Evans took a seat opposite him. His wife disappeared into the kitchen, but this time it was not to brew a pot of tea and offer Ladyfingers.

"We were about to leave," Phillip lied. "I hope this won't take long."

"Sir, we, my wife and I, were expecting you to give us an answer. We need your decision." Chen raised his voice an octave. "The test can't wait forever."

Chen's admonition angered Phillip. "My wife and I have reached a fork in the road. She wants to give permission for the DNA test, but she's not ready to take on the responsibility of caring for Marcie and the baby. I feel the same. I have wanted this climb to a life in politics since I was in college. I'm not about to give that up to deal with a kid that never listened to me in the first place."

Phillip Evan's words were bitter and sliced through Chen's heart like a mill saw slicing through the softest pinewood. "Can I take that as a yes?" Chen waited.

Marsha Evans could be seen from the corner of Chen's eye, standing behind the kitchen door. She was listening to every word, yet she refused to appear.

Mr. Evans grunted. He cleared his throat and paused. He appeared to be giving it a second thought. "You go ahead and apply for guardianship, Mr. Young. We can't take on the responsibility of a mother and baby at this time."

It was now clearer to Chen than when he first met Marcie's parents. They were the selfish and self-absorbed parents of a girl who had been misunderstood by them and abused by another. *The only good thing coming from all this is that we get Marcie and Grace Rose, and we can give them a good life.*

"Is there anything else?" Mr. Evans asked.

"Of course, this has to be done legally. I will have the papers processed as soon as I get back to the office. After the papers are filed, a court hearing will be scheduled, and you will be notified as to the time and date of the hearing."

Chen searched Marcie's father's eyes. He saw nothing but the cold, callous gaze of an uninterested father. He bid the man goodbye.

~~~

Niki was getting ready to go into town. She checked in on Marcie and Grace Rose before glancing out the window. She noticed Chen pulling the car into the driveway. She grabbed her purse and rushed out the door to greet him. "How did you make out?" Niki yelled. She ran to the car.

"We won, Nik, I'm so grateful, we won!"

Niki opened the driver's side door and hugged Chen. They held hands and said a prayer of thanksgiving to the Lord.

Chen handed Niki the car keys. "I'm going in to call Chief Dugan. I'll let him know what took place and ask him to help with the paperwork. The faster we apply, the faster we can get the test done."

"I won't be long. I'm running a few errands and making a stop to see Mrs. Brandywine on the way home. I have a feeling she needs uplifting," Niki said. Chen smiled.

Niki kissed Chen on the cheek and slipped into the driver's seat. She waved. "See you later," she said, as she backed out of the driveway and hung a left toward town.

Chen wanted to talk to Marcie before contacting Chief Dugan. He wanted to be sure she was okay with them going ahead with the guardianship plans. They had invested in her life so far, but she was young, and the young tend to change their minds more often than their elders. He would wait for Niki to return. He grabbed a quick lunch, a sandwich and a mug with coffee. After eating, he topped off his coffee and went directly to his study, carrying the mug with him.

Chen sat in his green chair and picked up the receiver. He dialed Darrell Dugan's number. "Chief Dugan here," was heard at the other end.

"Chief this is Pastor Young. I wanted to let you know, I returned to the Evanses' home this morning. Mr. Evans agreed to have Niki and I sponsor Marcie and Grace Rose. We want to file the papers for guardianship, so we can move on with the DNA testing." Chen paused. There was no response. "Chief are you there?" Chen asked.

"I'm thinking."

"What's the next step?"

"We could have the court draw up the papers and have Marcie's parents sign them, but I think you should hire a lawyer, one of your own choosing, instead of a court appointed one. You will have a better chance of moving the process along without any glitches."

Niki arrived home in time to cook dinner. Chen approached her and told her what Chief Dugan had suggested. "I'll put up a request for a reference on the church bulletin board on Sunday," she said. Let's hope we find a good lawyer and we can move things along."

~~~

Sunday came and brought with it torrential rains. Many congregants decided not to travel in the "monsoon," as Niki had called it, and they opted to stay home. Chen made his sermon shorter to the delight of the congregants who showed up.

Niki remembered to put in a request for a reference and pinned it to the bulletin board hanging in the entrance hall of the church.

~~~

It was seven p.m. Marcie and Grace Rose had retired to their room. Niki was busy settling the kitchen. The phone rang in Chen's study. "Hello, this is Reverend Young."

"Hello, Reverend, this is Chester Davis. I attended your church service today, and I saw the request for a lawyer on your message board. I would like to offer you my services, pro bono."

They were words directly from heaven. "Mr. Davis, that would be wonderful. Can we arrange a meeting? Would sometime this week be good for you? We can discuss the case then."

"You name the time and place, and I will be there. By the way, Reverend, your sermon hit home with me. Thank you."

~~~

The rest of the week flew. Chen had scheduled a meeting with Chester Davis for Thursday at one o'clock, at the parsonage.

Chester Davis was on time—to the minute. He entered Chen's study with the smile of a lawyer who had just won a case. Chen took a seat behind his desk and extended his hand to Chester. The two men greeted each other with a strong handshake. "Please have a seat," Chen pointed.

"Now why don't we start from the beginning. You talk, Pastor Young, I'll listen." Chester made strong eye contact with Chen. His tone was respectful.

Chen recognized the lawyer's sincerity. He conveyed a willingness to help.

Chen relayed to Chester all that had occurred since the day Marcie walked into his office. He explained that her parents had agreed to give up guardianship of their daughter and granddaughter, but Marcie's mother was absent from the conversation, and he didn't trust that. He felt a personal lawyer would be able to go through the loopholes, should there be any.

"What if Marcie's mother changes her mind?" Chen asked. "She heard the conversation from another room, but she refused to be a part of it." In frustration, Chen clenched his jaw.

"I have seen this before, Reverend. I will have the petitions drawn up, and I will bring them to Marcie's parents to sign. I will take two colleagues from my law firm with me. I will ask them to witness their signatures. There is not much they can do after everything is legalized in court. Don't concern yourself, we will take care of everything."

Chester Davis rose to his feet and shook hands with Chen. He reached the office door and turned. "My treat," he said. He smiled and showed himself out.

## CHAPTER THIRTY-TWO
(Kowloon - The Long Journey 1997)

Some years after the Kowloon trial, Li Young had signed a contract with Vincenzo Moncini, of Moncini Originals of Milan. He had discussed their encounter with no one, not even his wife, Hua. He blamed it on his reserved nature, for hiding their good fortune, but he knew that keeping her in the dark about their future was wrong. He told himself, he didn't want to get her hopes up. He was pacified. He decided to wait.

During the years that followed his acquittal, Li and Hua continued to work, saving every penny. From time to time Li would send his sketches to Moncini who transformed them into a lucrative market for men's apparel. Moncini took full credit for Li's designs. However, Li was steadfast. He wasn't looking for fame, and he was grateful for the extra money that would pave their way to America.

~~~

Great Britan transferred their sovereignty over Hong Kong to China, on July 1, 1997. It was the year that Li and Hua Young decided to make the move to the United States. They had lived through the riots of the Cultural Revolution and the Star Ferry passenger crossing. They had heard of the massacre in Beijing, in Tiananmen Square, where nearly ten thousand were slaughtered. Now China had taken control of their beloved island. They had had it. They would make the journey to America. It was time!

Prior to their journey, Li confessed about the success of his sketches to his wife. When he told her, she was supportive and thankful. Because of Li's relationship with Vincenzo Moncini, their dream to move to America would now become a reality.

Li hadn't told Chen and Niki about his dealings with the famous designer. He wanted to surprise them. Moncini had a new clothing line that would come out after the new year, and he would incorporate all of Li's designs. Li had settled for one lump sum for his original sketches, but any new designs he would come up with in the future were to be paid separately. His family would be set for life.

~~~

Fall seemed to have arrived unexpectedly. It was one week before Li and Hua would fly to the United States. The Youngs were packing, but it wasn't much. Their possessions were minimal. Hua was busy wrapping picture frames and the few breakables she possessed in plastic wrap. They had bought their tickets and obtained the necessary papers they needed. They were ready to go.

Their neighbor, Serena, who lived one floor above, stopped in to say goodbye. She was the only friend Hua had made at the low-rise. Serena was from the States and spoke fluent Cantonese. She taught English in a primary school on the Kowloon Peninsula.

Serena had started teaching Hua English words, when they had first met. Hua would teach her husband a word or two each day, and he was starting to grasp a little of the language. Before leaving for work, Hua would write the words Serena taught her on a piece of paper and tape it onto the refrigerator, so Li would see it when he arrived home.

"I have a gift for you to take to America." Serena handed Hua a package wrapped in colorful paper and tied with a blue ribbon.

Hua took the gift from her friend. "Thank you, so very much," Hua said in English. Serena beamed.

Hua loosened the ribbon and pulled on the paper wrapping. She opened the gift and was delighted to see it was a leather book of translation, from the Cantonese language to English. Hua's tears blurred the gift she held in her hand. "I will treasure your gift and think of you each time I read it." Hua opened the book to its first pages. "This will help a lot." The two women hugged and said their goodbyes.

Hua refused to pack the book Serena had given her. Hua tucked it away in her carry-on, and she looked at it often on the plane.

~~~

Tao and Bo Nguyen picked up Li and Hua before the scheduled time, in case they had last minute errands to attend to. They planned on taking a slower route to the airport so the Youngs could bid their last goodbyes to the island.

As they entered the car Li and Hua took one last look at the low-rise apartment they had lived in for so many years, its many windows reflecting the Asian sun. They shielded their eyes as they looked skyward. Serena was at the fourth floor window, waving goodbye. The couple waved back and stepped into the car, never to gaze at the low-rise again.

The Youngs were driven past the Quarry and Queen Victoria bays, with a full view of the water. It was like staring into a sheet of smooth glass. They saw the sampans and the larger fishing boats as they passed each other in a sea of blue calmness, while hungry gulls circled overhead. They saw the fishermen on the bridge and watched as they casted their lines hoping to catch a trophy, and they heard the fog horns as they blasted their last song. They eyed the passing images, as if they were watching an old film or turning the pages of a vintage family album. It prompted the pangs of nostalgia to tug at their hearts.

"Would you mind if I opened the window?" Li asked Tao.

"If you like. Some people prefer the open window instead of the air conditioning—please do."

Li opened the window. He could hear the sound of sampans brushing against the pilings of the pier. He caught glimpses of motorized rickshaws gliding down the alleys near the bay, as smooth as a professional skater glides across the ice. Unpopular among the locals, these modernized cabs maintained their tarpaulin roofs, some decorated with gold fringe that fluttered in the light breeze that was sweeping through the open window.

In the far distance Li could see the prison he had endured for many months, still standing high on the Kowloon bluff where he left it. Its red brick facade stood erect and tall, a reminder of the time he had endured there. He thought of how many innocent men may have been incarcerated because of false testimonies given by the Chang Chaos of the world. His heart skipped a beat. Until the image vanished, he continued to gaze. He stifled his tears. He did not look back.

The couple felt a pang of sadness as they gazed upon the lower hills. Would they ever again see the wildcats that roamed freely, or the monkeys, or the lace winged butterflies with their orange backs and their edges trimmed in black and white, resembling the finest tulle?

Further ahead they could see the clouds as they danced atop the higher peaks as if they were performing before the golden sun.

~~~

The Youngs arrived at Kai Tak Airport in time for check in and boarding, and the adrenaline was kicking in. Li had taken a motion sickness remedy an hour before; it was a recipe passed down by his parents, made with ginger root. Hua had refused. She suspected there was a sleep tonic in it. She didn't want to miss a moment!

The Nguyens exited the car and helped Li and Hua with their luggage. The couples hugged each other as they said goodbye, and Li and Hua thanked them for the ride. As they parted for the last time Bo stepped closer to Hua and whispered in her ear, "I'm pregnant." What a wonderful thought to leave their beloved Hong Kong with. Both women embraced and cried.

~~~

The flight proved to be stressful. A baby cried non-stop, and the man seated behind Hua coughed throughout the flight. Hua wished he had seen a doctor before he boarded the plane. Hua tried to divert her attention to the book Serena had given her. It helped, but not much.

Li and Hua Young arrived at John F. Kennedy Airport, on Tuesday, November 11, 1997. The plane landed on time, and out of the 245 passengers on the plane, two were unable to stop the flow of tears. They went directly to baggage claim and retrieved their luggage.

Chen and Niki were standing in the waiting area with a large sign that said: Welcome to America Li and Hua Young. His parents caught a glimpse of them from the glass window that separated the travelers from the visitors. Li and Hua couldn't exit the area fast enough. They ran toward each other, the four embracing, holding one another for several minutes before heading to the parking area.

Chen and Niki carried their luggage and led them to the tan Toyota.

It was a holiday in America. It was Veterans Day. It was also rush hour. The Belt Parkway was bumper-to-bumper. The downpour didn't make it any better. Headlights went on and windshield wipers hummed. Veterans wearing pinned hats, trying to sell poppy flowers, took cover beneath the overpasses, as the heavy rain pelted against the Toyota's windows. Chen leaned toward the dashboard and switched the defogger on. It barely helped.

Li and Hua were used to tropical storms, and the heavy traffic went unnoticed. They couldn't have cared less. They remained wide eyed as they took in what they could see of the landscape. The wide roads, stone tunnels, strip malls and the many gas stations amazed them. They were joyful to be home in America.

Despite the rain, the Young family pulled up to the parsonage a bit earlier than Chen had expected. He parked the car under the willow tree, and Niki hurried into the house to set a fire in the potbelly stove. It would remain chilly, well into the night.

Niki ran upstairs to check the guest bedroom. Were there enough towels, wash cloths, and blankets to make Chen's parents comfortable? Was the parsonage warm enough? Would they like her cooking? How long would they stay in her home? These recurring thoughts haunted her like a broken record.

Niki planned to share her time willingly with Hua. She would include her in church functions, and she would ask Hua's help in running the church programs. At twilight they could take long walks through the meadow and woodlands to the stream, chatting along the way—and back. They could have picnics in the nearby park, inviting others to come along. Niki would ask Hua to teach her how to make Chinese dishes and to teach her new words in Cantonese.

Although her mind was full of questions, Niki felt blessed. They had now become one family. The past and the present were now intertwined, and they were whole.

## CHAPTER THIRTY-THREE
(The Signatures 2002)

Chester Davis was sitting in his office on Camwood's east side, a few blocks north of China Town. His partner, Henry Travis, and his legal secretary, Wanita Horn, were present. They moved to an inner room and sat at a long mahogany conference table. They eased into the black leather chairs on wheels. Chester closed the door for privacy.

Chester picked up a large glass pitcher and poured iced water with lemon slices into two tall tumblers. His colleagues accepted the drinks and listened intently to what he had to say. He filled them in on the Marcie Evans case.

Both colleagues knew Phillip Evans. They had dealings with him before, remembering him, not his wife Marsha. They admitted they didn't know the boy involved in Marcie's case.

Henry had heard through the town grapevine that Phillip Evans, Marcie's father, was going to run for assemblyman if the boy's father, Andrew Boylan, stepped down to run a campaign for governor of the state. It didn't surprise them that Phillip Evans would exchange a relationship with his daughter for notoriety and power. "That's what power does to you," Chester said, with sadness.

Chester explained to them that one of their colleagues had been sent to Washington, D.C. "I'd like you to accompany me to the Evanses' home. I'll give them a call in the morning. The sooner we get this done, the sooner the DNA test will be processed." Henry and Wanita agreed to go.

~~~

The following morning brought with it cloudy skies. Chester rose early. He shaved and showered. He chose to look super professional, wearing a gray pinstripe suit with a matching vest. He chose a gray and purple tie with diagonal stripes, worn over a starched white shirt, and he placed a deep purple handkerchief in his jacket pocket. As he bent down to tie his laces, his Italian black leather shoes reflected the form of his clean shaven face. He looked every bit the professional.

Henry Travis and Wanita Horn were to meet him in front of the Evanses' home at 10:00 a.m. sharp. Chester arrived first. He waited in front of the white clapboard house, going over the legal papers to transfer Marcie's guardianship to Chen and Niki Young. The Evanses were expecting him.

At 10:15 a.m., a car pulled up behind Chester's. He could see Henry and Wanita through the rearview mirror. They stepped out of the car and approached the driver's side of Chester's red four door sedan. "We're here," Henry announced.

Chester's neck was tense. He raised his eyebrows. "I can see that! Let's get going. I want to get this over with."

The trio approached the front entrance, and Chester rang the bell. Phillip Evans opened the door and asked them to step in. "I didn't know you were bringing your entourage with you," he said, squinting and leaving one long line between his eyes. "Let's make this fast, I have a busy day."

"I'm sorry I didn't mention it. I will make it brief."

Chester eyed Marsha Evans. She was standing behind the kitchen door, as she had done before, listening to every word.

"Will you please come in here," Phillip shouted. "You need to be a part of this." He asked the trio to sit.

Chester raised his voice. "We need your signature, Mrs. Evans."

There was silence for nearly half a minute. Marsha Evans appeared in the doorway and walked into the living area. Her jaw was tense, and she tightened her lips. *She may not sign,* Chester thought. "I'm here!" Marsha said.

"Good. Now let's get started," Chester demanded, as a teacher would scold his class for being late.

"These are the papers you need to sign," Chester explained. "After the petitions are filed, there will be a court hearing before a judge. You have up until that time to change your mind. The Youngs will become the guardians of Marcie and Grace Rose, if the judge votes in their favor. Until Marcie reaches the age of eighteen, that is."

Chester handed Phillip Evans the papers. "Being you haven't asked your attorney for advice, I am filing the release for you. Wanita will notarize it this morning."

Chester waited while Phillip and Marsha completed the paperwork. Phillip signed the papers in the places the lawyer requested. He wasted no time. *My daughter will soon be of age and that will get rid of the Youngs once and for all,* Phillip surmised. He would be able to run his campaign without guilt.

Marsha took her time. *The Youngs will be in charge for only a short time!* Her thoughts were pacified. *Until this is settled in court, I can contest the guardianship.* She took the pen from Chester, and she signed her daughter into the care of the Youngs. Her hand trembled as she signed on the dotted lines.

Wanita notarized the papers and bid the Evanses goodbye. She and Henry would not stay a minute longer. They showed themselves out. Chester Davis shook hands with Phillip, and Marsha disappeared into the kitchen, with no response.

Once outside, Chester thanked his colleagues for being there.

"If that were my child, I wouldn't have signed so fast," Wanita said. "Did you notice, Mr. Evans didn't stop for a moment to think about it?"

"All he could think of is he'd be free to run a campaign, without distraction," Henry commented.

"Let's hope neither of them change their minds. Now we have to wait," Chester offered. "Once the petitions are filed with the county clerk, they will issue a court date. See you back at the office."

## CHAPTER THIRTY-FOUR
(Next Case 2002)

Chester Davis Esq. walked up the marble steps to the courthouse, north of Washington Street. He was wearing a brown herringbone suit, a double-breasted vest, a white shirt, and a brown and beige tie and looked every bit the lawyer he was. He had checked his briefcase before leaving his home to make sure all the signed papers were in order. He notified Wanita and Henry he was on his way. They were to meet him in the court lobby at 8:00 a.m.

Hoping the day would go smooth without any glitches, Chester pulled on the brass handle of the 12 ft. mahogany and glass door and whispered a simple prayer. He placed his car keys, his watch, and his tie clip in a basket that passed through a metal detector. He retrieved his belongings and was directed to the reception desk.

The court lobby was long and wide. There were black and white marble tiles diagonally covering the floor. A large blue and gray marble emblem of the county's crest was embossed in its center.

Murals depicting the assembling of our forefathers covered the walls. Images of George Washington, Abraham Lincoln, Thomas Jefferson, and Benjamin Franklin, along with many others, discussing and forming the doctrines and principles that would protect the rights of every American and keep them safe. The murals had faded with age, now resembling pastel watercolors, instead of vivid acrylics or deep rich oils. The images had faded, but their beauty and meaning had withstood time.

A cherrywood rectangular desk stood in the middle of the room, flanked by the American flag on one side and the state and county flags on the other side.

A robust woman sat behind the reception desk. She had gray hair and large powder blue eyes. She greeted all who approached the desk, inquiring why they were there and directing them to the proper courtrooms where their cases would be heard.

Chester Davis approached the desk. "Good morning, how can I direct you today?" The woman asked.

She had a sweet spirit, he thought, and her smile was comforting. The butterflies in his stomach ceased for a moment and he smiled back. "I'm here to attend to a case in Probate Court."

"Name of the judge presiding?"

"Judge Adam Wise."

"One moment." The greeter checked her copies of the day's schedule. The names of the judges presiding were in alphabetical order. She slid her index finger down the page until she reached the judge's name and location of the courtroom where the case was to be heard. "You're to take the elevator to the second floor, turn right and its several doors on your left. All the courtrooms have signs to the right of their doors, you can't miss it. The sign will say: Probate Court. You're scheduled for 8:30 a.m." "You're first on Judge Wise's docket," she added. She smiled.

"Thank you." Chester returned the smile and walked back to the entrance doors. He waited for nearly fifteen minutes. Wanita and Henry were nowhere in sight. He checked his watch, and he decided to wait in the courtroom. He turned and walked in the direction of the elevators.

Once he reached the second floor, Chester paused. The hallway was long and narrow. Each doorway was framed in thick dark mahogany, with added decorative moldings far above their casings. Their hinges and hardware were shiny brass.

White globular lighting fixtures were mounted to the right of each door frame, reminding Chester of the old schoolhouse fixtures from his elementary school days. He walked about twenty feet and stood before a door, on his left. The brass sign next to the door said: PROBATE COURT.

Before he entered the courtroom, Chester whispered a quick prayer. He was directed by the bailiff to be seated on the left side of the room to await the judge's entrance.

Chen and Niki Young had arrived earlier, with Marcie and Grace Rose at their side. They were seated in the front of the room opposite the bench. Chen was dressed in a basic gray suit. He wore a white shirt and a striped purple and gray silk Jacquard tie.

Niki had dressed simply in a sapphire blue shirtwaist dress. She wore a pink patent leather belt tied around her small waist. Her shoes and bag matched the belt.

Niki rarely wore foundation makeup, and this day was no exception. Her sun kissed complexion had a sprinkle of tan freckles across her cheeks and the bridge of her nose. She had brushed a whisper of pale pink blush on her high cheek bones, and she added a deeper pink lipstick to her full lips. Her shoulder length auburn hair glowed under the overhead lights, creating an aura about her. She looked like an angel.

Chester Davis greeted the Youngs and gave Marcie a hug. He picked up Grace Rose who smiled at him. Her little fingers reached out as if she were trying to grab the handkerchief in his breast pocket. Her smile radiated, and she giggled as the lawyer put her back in her mother's arms.

Marcie was dressed in a medium length A-line dress, made of dotted Swiss material. The color was a deep ecru. She wore yellow leather flat shoes and a matching purse. She looked like a child. Niki had made the dress for her with leftover material she had when sewing Marcie's maternity outfits, and Marcie insisted on wearing it. It was one of her favorites.

Reluctant to come Marcie was still. She sat with her hands in her lap, curling and uncurling her fingers. Her stomach fluttered, and her mouth was dry. She had refused breakfast when Niki offered it. "I'll eat when this is over," she told Niki.

The seats were long oak benches that resembled church pews. As Chester sat, his memory jolted to his youth when he attended church faithfully with his parents. He hadn't walked into a church in twenty years until he attended Chen's church and heard the sermon that pierced his heart. His image faded.

Chester turned his head and looked in the direction of the entrance door. Wanita and Henry were nowhere in sight. The butterflies returned to Chester's stomach. He sat quiet for a few moments and turned his head again when he heard the door open.

People began to file in and fill up the seats until one half of the courtroom was occupied. The Youngs' case was the first case to be heard that morning.

Phillip and Marsha Evans entered the courtroom and were directed to the right side, facing the judge's bench. Phillip walked ahead of his wife while Marsha walked slower, as a bridesmaid would pace herself to the altar. They nodded to Chester, and he nodded back. Chester wondered why Marsha decided to come. He hadn't expected her to show up.

Judge Adam Wise opened the door to his chambers and walked to the bench. He was a tall man with salt and pepper hair and unassuming espresso eyes as small as coffee beans. He wore tortoise shell glasses, and his eyebrows and mustache, unlike his hair, were jet black. A thought crossed Chester's mind that the judge might dye them. He wore a long black robe and a wide smile. He nodded to the bailiff who shouted, "All rise, this Court is now in session."

Henry Travis and Wanita Horn came barreling through the door. They were approached by the bailiff and directed to a bench behind Chester who turned and scowled. "Sorry, we got tied up in traffic," Henry whispered.

"I'm sure you did," Chester pontificated.

The bailiff instructed Henry and Wanita to remain seated. They sat quietly during the entire Court session. They waited to be called upon. They were not.

To prevent any gossip from hurting his campaign, if Phillip were to run for assemblyman, the Evanses chose not to bring their lawyer along.

Chen glanced over and thought Marsha looked no different than the last time he had seen her. She was poorly dressed, and he wondered why she hadn't worn her slippers with the fake fur. Her husband looked neater in a blue suit and a white shirt, but he wore no tie. Chen thought, for a future assemblyman he could have been better dressed.

Chester saw the Evanses were alone. He would rather a lawyer represent them now, when he was charged up, then to have them hire someone down the line to throw a wrench into the proceedings.

"Good morning," the Judge's deep voice resounded. The Youngs' case was to be called first. "Let's proceed." The Judge motioned for Chester to approach the bench.

"Good Morning, Your Honor," Chester answered. The Evanses sat stoically, as the lawyer approached the bench and handed Judge Wise the signed documents.

Judge Wise took his time and went over every word of the signed petitions. "I see your clients are requesting guardianship of a one, Marcie Evans, and her daughter, Grace Rose, is that correct?" he asked. Chester nodded. "Are they here in this courtroom today?" the Judge asked.

"Yes, Your Honor, I'm representing them." Chester turned toward the Youngs and back to the Judge. "The parents of Marcie Evans have agreed to the transfer of their daughter's guardianship to my clients, Reverend Chen Young, and his wife, Nicole Young."

Judge Wise motioned for Chen and Niki to step forward. His eyes pointed to Marcie who was holding Grace Rose, and he nodded. Marcie also rose and stood before the Judge. "Mr. and Mrs. Evans will you approach the bench," he ordered.

Phillip and Marsha stepped up to the bench, without expression. Judge Wise glanced at the Youngs and motioned for them to move closer.

Judge Wise addressed Marcie's parents. "You have both have agreed to transfer guardianship of your daughter, Marcie Evans, to the Reverend here and his wife, Nicole Young. Is that correct?" the Judge asked. "That also includes guardianship of your granddaughter, Grace Rose."

Phillip and Marsha answered, "Yes."

During the proceedings, neither one of Marcie's parents looked at her or Grace Rose. They kept their eyes focused on the judge.

Both Chen and Niki had hoped the Evanses, upon seeing their daughter and granddaughter in court, would have a change of heart toward them. As much as they wanted Marcie and Grace Rose to stay with them, Chen and Niki knew it would be the right thing for the Evanses to do. It was clear that wouldn't happen, at least not today. Marcie, however, had no high expectations. She had accepted what was a long time ago, and she was resigned to it.

Judge Wise leaned in. He held his chin high, making eye contact with Phillip and Marsha Evans. "I see you did not seek your own legal counsel and have agreed to go ahead with the proceedings. I will warn you that after today you will not be able to resume guardianship of your daughter, Marcie, and her daughter, Grace Rose. Once Marcie turns eighteen, she can do as she pleases. Do you understand what I've said?"

"Yes, Your Honor, we do." Phillip Evans answered.

The Judge looked deep into Marsha's eyes. He waited. "Yes, Your Honor."

"Okay, it's settled. The guardianship of Marcie Evans has been given to Reverend Chen Young and his wife, Nicole Young, until Marcie Evans reaches the age of eighteen years old. That includes guardianship of Marcie's infant daughter, Grace Rose."

"There's additional paperwork that needs to be processed," the Judge added, "but that will not change the outcome of today's decision." He waited.

The Evanses nodded. At the mention of her name, the grandparents of Grace Rose showed no emotion.

Judge Wise looked upon the couples standing before the bench. He smiled at Marcie and Grace Rose and banged the gavel hard on its sound block. He shouted, "next case!"

## CHAPTER THIRTY-FIVE
### (The Test 2002)

It had been several days since the court had granted Chen and Niki guardianship of Marcie and her daughter, Grace Rose. The following Monday morning, Chen contacted Darrel Dugan.

Chief Dugan had exited the elevator to begin his shift. He could hear the phone resonating from his office. He raced to his desk and picked up the receiver on the last ring. "Hello this is Chief Dugan."

"Chief this is Reverend Chen Young. You sound a bit winded, I'm sorry if I made you rush."

"No problem, Reverend, I've been meaning to call you. I haven't been able to reach the Evans family. What can I do for you today?"

"I'm calling to let you know we went to court last week. We have been granted legal guardianship of Marcie and Grace Rose. We are now responsible for them, and we would like to go forward with the DNA testing as soon as possible. Being you had contacted Dr. Gorden in the past, we were hoping you could arrange for him to come to the parsonage and perform the test here. Marcie requested it be done at home."

"I'll get right on it Reverend. I'll get back to you today."

Both men hung up the phone, and Chief Dugan placed a call to Dr. Neil Gorden on his private line. He left the doctor a message and waited for a return call.

It took under three minutes and the phone rang. "Chief Dugan here."

"Chief Dugan, this is Dr. Gorden. I received your message. I'm unable to come myself. I have to finish my rounds and return to the office. I have long hours today. I am sending a technician from the hospital to draw Grace Rose's blood. She will be there today, although I can't give you the exact time. Will you please advise the family to be ready for the technician."

"I'm on it," Darrell answered.

"Before you hang up, I have to warn you, this test, because it is being done at home, may not be admissible in a court of law. There are strict chain of custody procedures that must be followed. However, my lawyer has advised me that it will establish the paternity of Grace Rose. If you can convince Marcie to have the test done in a lab, I will cancel the technician for today. If I don't hear from you by noon, I will send her over to the parsonage."

"Thank you, Doctor. Marcie has made it very clear; She wants nothing to do with the father of Grace Rose."

"If in the future she should change her mind, she may have to have the test repeated in a lab," the doctor advised.

Darrell placed a call to the parsonage. No one was there to answer it. He left a message and hoped the Youngs or Marcie would receive it in time and not be surprised when the technician showed up at the door.

~~~

Marcie was in the kitchen preparing Grace Rose's lunch, when the doorbell rang. Chen had received the message and Marcie was expecting the visit. She greeted the technician and ushered her into the living area. She introduced herself as Brittany.

The day was damp. It had rained during the night. Niki had risen early and went down to the living area to light a fire in the cast iron stove. The room was warm and ready to receive the technician.

Marcie had been offered a non-invasive DNA test for Grace Rose. Chen and Niki had requested a blood test, but they wanted Grace's mother to make the final decision. The three considered the options for several days. They reasoned drawing the infant's blood would be the most accurate.

Marcie made sure that Grace Rose had her morning nap so she wouldn't be cranky. She was bright eyed and smiling when her mother introduced her.

Marcie led Brittany to a table in the living area, where she could set up her medical equipment. There wasn't much to lay out. She took alcohol swabs, lancets, and capillary tubing from her medical satchel and placed them on the table. Brittany had also brought butterfly needles and a small tourniquet, along with different size tubing, in case Grace Rose's size required a venipuncture. When she observed Grace Rose, she realized a heel prick was all that was necessary. Marcie was relieved.

Marcie had done her homework. She offered to warm a diaper to place on Grace Rose's foot, before the test; This would improve the circulation to her heel. Brittany declined. She had brought heel warmers with her. She wrapped one around the infant's heel and left to wash up in the bathroom.

Brittany returned and removed the heel warmer. She donned surgical gloves and swabbed Grace's tiny heel with an alcohol swab. She allowed the area to dry. She gently lifted the baby's heel and pressed the lancet into its side. Grace Rose howled, but stopped for a few seconds when Marcie showed her one of her favorite toys. It was a stuffed lamb.

Brittany was gentle, as she wiped the first drop of blood away with sterile gauze. She collected the sample into a small capillary tube. After she was sure she had extracted the right amount, she capped the tube. She swabbed the area and placed sterile gauze on the perforation site, holding it there for a minute. Finally, she covered the area with a sterile pad.

Brittany removed a sharps container from her medical carry-on and discarded the lancet. She labeled the tube and placed it into the container. She wiped the table's surface with a sanitized cleanser, removed her gloves and discarded them. She disappeared into the bathroom to wash her hands.

Grace Rose grabbed the toy and clung to its soft curls, holding tight. Her little chest slowly stopped heaving up and down, and her cries trickled down to a whimper.

Brittany returned and walked to the sofa. She sat to complete her paperwork. She told Marcie to expect the results of the test within a week. If there were any delay, she would be notified.

Marcie thanked the technician and walked her to the door. By this time Grace Rose was giggling, forgetting altogether the pain she had endured.

Chen and Niki walked into the kitchen and smiled. "Now we wait Marcie. In a few days we will be able to declare who the father of Grace Rose is, and so must the Boylans."

## CHAPTER THIRTY-SIX
### (Transitions)

Li and Hua Young's transition to life in a foreign land had gone as smooth as the marble terraces in the summer palaces of Beijing. They adapted well to the customs of their new country, and it wasn't long before they felt America was their homeland. They had become true patriots. However, the most meaningful transition for them was that they had become Christians.

~~~

Chen had come to know Christ several years before his parents. He had written them often, telling them of his conversion. By the words their son wrote Li and Hua had noticed a change in him. He was happier and more peaceful than they had ever known him to be. His reactions were different. His relationship with God was one of trust.

Li and Hua began to question their own beliefs. "Who is this new God he follows?" they would ask each other. "Chen says He is alive." They had never known other gods to come back from the grave. Those idols were dead!

Chen explained to them that his God was indeed alive, and the gospels attested to it. Jesus had paid the price for their sin—for all sin, by the shedding of His blood. It was a once and for all sacrifice; A free gift! They only had to believe and accept it. "It is finished," Jesus had cried out as He gave up His last breath. His resurrection would follow, giving hope and joy to all generations. The price for sin had been paid in full. The Youngs began to see and understand. The scales had been removed from their eyes.

~~~

Li and Hua had grown to love Marcie and Grace Rose. They would babysit with joy whenever Marcie had to run errands in town or when they watched Grace Rose in the church's nursery during choir practice. Grace would eye her mother on a screen that was set up in the playroom, and she would check on it from time to time, making sure her mother was nearby.

Li and Hua had also grown to love Samuel and considered him a younger son—one they could dote on.

The Young family had grown into an extended one; one with no differences. God was their Father, and they were His children. That's what it amounted to, and it couldn't have been a sweeter existence!

## CHAPTER THIRTY-SEVEN
### (The Results 2002)

Dr. Neil Gorden sat at his office desk, picked up the receiver and placed a call to the Young household. The results of Grace Rose's DNA test was in, and Dr. Gorden wanted no middleman. He left a message for the Youngs to make an appointment with his office at their convenience. He would give them the results of the lab report then.

Chen and Niki brought the news to Marcie. "You go in my behalf. I don't want to be there, I already know who the father is!" Marcie's bitterness was understood. Chen and Niki questioned it no further.

"We will be happy to represent you," Chen offered.

~~~

The Youngs arrived a few minutes before the scheduled time. Dr. Gorden was running late. They would wait.

The waiting room was packed. Mothers with new arrivals were there for their first appointment, and the cries of newborns could be heard down the hallway. Some were hungry, some wet, some hot, and some cold. The tired ones were being rocked to sleep. A few hungry babies were being nursed or bottle fed.

On the other side of the room, babies were coughing and in need of medication. A partition separated them from the well babies.

It was after one o'clock when Dr. Gorden walked into the building. He used the rear door, adjacent to the parking area. He slipped quietly into his office. He opened the monitor and saw the Youngs seated in the waiting room.

He spoke over the intercom and asked one of his staff to show them in.

Dr. Gorden's grip was firm as he greeted the Youngs. He went behind his wide walnut desk and sat. He opened a manila envelope his secretary had placed on his desk that morning, and he withdrew the lab report.

Chen and Niki felt sure of the results, so they didn't flinch. Not a bit! Dr. Gorden read the report to them, word for word. They remained calm. When he was finished, the couple whispered a prayer of thanksgiving to God.

The results were positive, and Richard Boylan was legally declared the father of Grace Rose.

~~~

The following day was a Friday. Chen had to run a few errands in town and thought he would stop by the chief's office. He wanted to reveal the result of the lab report to Darrell.

Chen knocked on Chief Dugan's door. He opened the door and stuck his head in. "Am I interrupting you," Chen asked.

"No, please come in, Reverend. I need a break." The two men shook hands. "Please sit, I'll send out for coffee if you like."

Chen declined the offer. "Niki and I saw Dr. Gorden yesterday. He gave us the results of the DNA test. The results were positive. Richard Boylan *is* the father of Grace Rose. Here is a copy of the report for your files. We have a signed release, and you can keep it for any future reference."

"You were right. Who's going to tell Boylans?" Darrell asked.

"We are leaving that up to Chester Davis our lawyer. He will pay them a visit this week. He will handle it." "What's in the future for the boy?" Chen asked.

"He committed a crime. If this goes further and he's convicted, he will be charged but as an adult, I doubt it. Some cases are."

"If he's not charged as an adult, what will happen to him?"

"You sound sorry for the boy, are you?"

"In a way. We all need forgiveness."

"We would have to leave it up to the court system. If they decide he is charged for rape as a minor, the juvenile court will take over." The chief hesitated for a moment. "Personally, I don't see how the Boylans can hide this. Court records are easily accessible. If Marcie agrees to proceed with the case, the DNA test may have to be repeated in a lab."

~~~

Chen returned to the parsonage. He parked beneath the willow tree and shut the motor. He thought of the scripture in Romans. He repeated the words written. "God causes all things to work together for good to those who love God, to those who are called according to His purpose." He thought of Marcie and Grace Rose.

## CHAPTER THIRTY-EIGHT
(The White Tent - Spring 2002)

It wasn't long after Li and Hua arrived in the United States that Li confided to Chen and Niki of his relationship with the designer from Milan, Vincenzo Moncini. From time to time Li would send Moncini his sketches, and he would be handsomely paid for each portfolio.

Vincenzo Moncini had benefited from Li's talent, for many years, and he knew it. He wanted to show his gratitude. Moncini's spring creations would be shown at Bryant Park, New York City, in January of 2002. However, he wanted Li to be recognized for his creativity and talent.

In the summer of 2001, Moncini spoke with the park officials about having Li show his designs at the opening of the following spring season, with enough time for consumers to buy and wear his fashions. The show would include Li's line of men's spring and summer attire, including coats, jackets, shirts, trousers, and summer shorts.

Once Moncini's plans were approved, he wrote Li and requested he design a complete line of men's fashions to debut at Bryant Park, New York City, in Spring 2002. He requested Li send him the designs at the beginning of the winter season, so Moncini could arrange construction of Li's sketches. They would discuss the types of fabrics and the colors Li would choose for each garment, along with stitching techniques and Li's choice of buttons and zippers. Moncini would arrange for the patterns to be drafted and the garments produced in record time, in order for Li to tell his story.

Vincenzo Moncini assured Li that he would be given full recognition for the clothing line, and he would walk the red carpet with him, behind the models, at the completion of the show. The show would be promoted and advertised worldwide, thanks to the connections Moncini had in the fashion industry.

Li wrote back, in English. He told Moncini that he would be honored.

~~~

Despite the facades of concrete and steel, spring in Manhattan had exploded with color. The red maples and the golden forsythia had already bloomed. The newest buds of lime green, which laid dormant all winter, dangled from the many species of trees like delicate bells, proudly announcing the beginning of a new season. The white tree blossoms of the Callery pears and crabapples, the lavender and pink blooms of the eastern rosebuds, and the delicate white petals of the hawthorns, with their dark pink centers, graced the nearby parks.

~~~

Bryant Park was abuzz with excitement. Li's spring fashion show was about to make its debut. Designers had come from all over the world to participate. Models were being fitted and backdrops created.

The Moncini catwalk was extended to reach three quarters of the giant white anchor tent's length the show was to be held under. Its white covering allowed the textures and colors of the new creations, worn by tall male models, to stand out among the spectators.

~~~

The Youngs and their guests had anticipated this event for months and received their tickets a month before the show. When sending the tickets Vincenzo Moncini had included Marcie, Grace Rose, Samuel, and his mother, Jeanette. His generosity included air fare and hotel expenses. Li's brother,

Benny, and his sister-in-law, Joy, would attend the show at their own expense, and they certainly could afford it.

~~~

The family chose the St. Regis Hotel, founded by John Jacob Astor in 1904. It was located on 55<sup>th</sup> Street, overlooking Fifth Avenue, in Midtown Manhattan. Its carpeted steps, with its red plush covering, led up to the revolving glass doors that were trimmed with brass and welcomed visitors from all parts of the world.

~~~

As they entered the hotel, a doorman greeted the Young family. Marcie looked above at the painted blue sky and the white clouds that resembled floating puffs of cotton. She saw murals surrounding the ceiling on either side of the massive lobby and a crystal and gold leaf chandelier that hung over the marble flooring. "I've never seen anything like it," she said. The others looked in awe; they were speechless.

"Wow!" Samuel said. His mother Jeanette marveled at the display of talent that made it all possible.

Li Young approached the concierge desk. Matthew Whyler was in charge. He was expecting Li and greeted him as he would a celebrity. "Mr. Young, we were expecting you. We see you have your family with you. I hope your fashion show is a great success. Enjoy your stay with us, we are honored to have you as a guest."

The gentleman handed Li a set of keys for each room his family members would occupy. Li smiled as he handed them out. He took nothing for granted, he savored every moment.

~~~

The family showered and dressed for dinner. From the second level they decided to walk down the opulent marble staircase, its brass banister turning with the steps in a gentle curve. Because she was carrying Grace Rose, Marcie chose to take the elevator.

They arrived in the dining room at seven p.m. There were no words to express the elegance they stepped into. *How can heaven be better than this?* Marcie wondered.

Chen observed the artistry in the room. He noticed Marcie's expression. Chen knew the power of God and His creativity, and he thought of the scripture: *'Things which eye has not seen and ear has not heard, and which have not entered the heart of man, all that God has prepared for those who love Him.'* He repeated the scripture to her. "God has so much more for us, Marcie," he said.

Crystal and brass chandeliers hung from the painted gold and white ceiling. There were vertical panels throughout the room trimmed in gold leaf and adorned with round crystal sconces. A large mirror stood on one wall. It was sectioned in sixteen squares, its image reflecting the massive fireplace on the opposite wall.

Some tables were round and large, accommodating seven to eight people. They were covered in crisp linen cloths. Each table was set with white and gold plates of fine china. White cloth napkins accompanied each setting. The glasses and vases were made of crystal. Each vase held a bouquet of pink, white, and lavender roses, placed in the center of each table. The room resembled a springfest, welcoming in the new season.

Marcie and Samuel giggled when they threatened to take off their shoes and feel the plush, whimsical carpeting beneath their feet. Its color was light lilac, mixed with white, and there were deep purple circles sprinkled about like sparkles on a birthday card. The drapery contrasted the room's decor with burgundy tie backs, topped with deep burgundy canopies centered in a light purple design.

The menu was as luxurious as the room. Marcie, Samuel, and Jeanette chose the three-cheese ravioli entrée. The rest of the family chose the shrimp and scallop combination. All seven chose the summer salad. They declined dessert.

~~~

After dinner the family decided to walk the few blocks to Central Park. The park was bursting with tourists of all ages, wanting to enjoy the cool spring air. As twilight hovered over the city, some visitors, along with the locals, spread their blankets over the lush green lawn of Sheep Meadow. They were hoping to see some stars, despite the city lights.

Marcie wanted Grace Rose to experience her first carousel ride. As they approached the merry-go-round, they were in awe of its size. Li had researched its history. His English had improved, but whatever he couldn't express Chen would translate from Cantonese.

"Marcie, did you know the original carousel was powered by a mule and a horse that stayed underground?" Marcie looked at Li squinted and shook her head. "The animals learned to start and stop the ride at the sound of the operators tapping foot above them," Li added. Marcie laughed. The image was foreign to Marcie but not to Li who was raised without the benefits of modern technology.

"The current carousel is an antique that has been restored several times. It's a color extravaganza. See the cherubs and the red beams that support the ceiling? There are lights attached that twinkle at night like a hundred stars." Li smiled at his narrative.

The horses and chariots were hand carved and hand painted. Marcie chose to sit in a chariot with Grace on her lap. She felt it was safer. As they twirled, the evening breeze swept through Marcie's chestnut locks. She took in the landscape of the lush green lawns and listened to the hum of guitars in the far distance. Spanish tourists were singing, wearing sombreros and the colorful costumes of their native country. Having never been outside of Camwood, Marcie felt she was living in a dream.

~~~

Twilight had turned to dark, and the lights of the carousel illuminated the night sky. Marcie turned to take one last look. As the ride twirled and the music played, her eyes were drawn to the red beams and the attached lights that sparkled. *Li is right,* Marcie thought, *the lights look like a hundred twinkling stars.* Her eyes also twinkled.

The family walked through the park for at least an hour. On their way back to the hotel, they passed Bow Bridge. The cast iron bridge was painted over in a light color, and its intricate design gave the look of carved stone.

An artist had set up easels next to the lake. Chen asked Marcie if she would like a portrait of Grace Rose drawn with chalk, in a deep shade of gray. Marcie was delighted but hesitated. Chen caught the look. "Marcie, we want you to have a reminder of your visit to New York, please let us bless you with it."

As they exited the park, Marcie held the portrait close to her breast. Chen failed to see the grateful tears welling up and slipping down her cheeks. She wiped them away as quickly as they fell.

There were many kiosks around. Some vendors selling cotton candy, others ice cream. One in particular was selling hot dogs. Having heard you should never leave New York City without having one of the city's hot dogs, Chen shouted out, "tomorrow we will have a picnic in the park, consisting of New York hot dogs with sauerkraut, onions in red sauce, mustard or ketchup—the works!" They laughed.

The family crossed Fifth Avenue. Chen approached a kiosk that was selling everything from newspapers to souvenirs. He bought Grace Rose a big red balloon. The infant squealed with delight as she tried to grasp its string.

~~~

The following morning, Li had an appointment to meet with Vincenzo Moncini at Bryant Park, to view Li's line of designs. The family rose early. They showered and dressed and took the elevator down to the dining room. Breakfast was being served. Having never enjoyed such pampering before, they all had the same look. Chen noticed their expressions. "When God blesses you, you thank Him. That's all there is to it! It's a gift He's given, and there should be no guilt attached to it. We are His children. We bless our own earthly family, don't we, and we are part of His family."

Li and Hua walked to Bryant Park with the rest of the family in tow. The family wanted to explore the New York Public Library which was situated on the next avenue, behind the park. Chen asked his father and mother to stand with him and pray, before Li embarked on the world of fashion; a world they knew nothing of. The family stood on the corner of Fifth Avenue and formed a circle of prayer. Passersby hardly noticed, as they hurried along to their destinations.

After they prayed Li and Hua entered the massive white canvas tent. Behind the tent, restaurant personnel were setting up chafing pans on long tables with fuel burners underneath. The staff would provide lunch during the days leading up to the fashion show, compliments of Vincenzo Moncini. Everyone would take advantage of the wonderful array of food they provided—except Li's models. They barely ate.

Li and Hua left the family and disappeared into the tent. Vincenzo Moncini was standing there with a wide grin to greet the couple. The others walked to the library to take in another wonder of the city.

~~~

Plans to build the New York Public Library began in the late 1800s, and its construction took nearly sixteen years to complete. It opened its doors to the public in 1911. As they approached the steps, the family marveled at the façade made of marble, brought in from the quarries of Vermont. They eyed the beautiful statues standing over Greek columns and the famous stately lions, carved from marble, that had greeted millions of visitors of past generations.

As soon as he saw the lions, Chen thought of Jesus. He smiled. They had a majestic look of power and strength. *No wonder He's called the Lion of Judah.* The family was awestruck.

Marcie picked up little Grace and sat her on one of the lions. She stood next to her daughter, holding her waist tight. Marcie asked Niki to take a picture, another token and reminder of her trip. Niki obliged. She smiled as she took several images.

Once inside they toured the many rooms. The ceilings were painted with sky and clouds, similar to the painted ceilings at the St. Regis. These ceilings were embellished with thick carvings surrounding them. The lamps on the tables were topped with gold metal shades, and the family was impressed with the low hanging chandeliers, their soft lights casting a yellow glow to the main reading room.

The Young family approached a librarian, who sat at a long mahogany desk. She was eager to answer any questions and ready to help retrieve a volume. Niki greeted the woman. "Good morning, we are visiting from out of town. We were wondering how many volumes are here at the library?"

The woman returned the greeting and smiled. She looked delightful, Marcie thought, *like the cotton candy on a stick, sold at the kiosks in Central Park.* She wore her pure white hair braided in a neat twist at the nape of her neck. Her braid was secured with an embellishment of colored crystals in the shape of a butterfly. She appeared to be in her early sixties. She was tall in stature and wore a lilac linen suit with large, round navy blue buttons. Marcie could not help but smile.

The librarian handed Niki a pamphlet with all the information she needed to tour the building. She looked over at the family, and her smile grew wider. Chen thought she had a twinkle in her eye. "There are millions of volumes here," she answered. "Any subject you are researching is at your fingertips. You only have to fill out a card and we will fetch it for you."

Niki thanked the woman, and they continued on with their tour of the building.

~~~

The Young family had planned an evening picnic in Central Park. Chen did a bit of shopping during the day and stopped in a small shop which sold everything from pots and pans to tablecloths. He purchased a large red and white plaid cloth used for outdoor picnics and bought a large brown wicker basket to hold the food. There were red plastic cups tucked into a side pocket of the basket.

Chen decided they would purchase their drinks from one of the kiosks. After their day of planning under the big white tent Li and Hua would join them.

~~~

Vincenzo Moncini had given Li carte blanche to choose the models for the fashion show and the formation in which his fashions would be presented. He interviewed about one hundred men, and out of them, he chose twelve models.

Each model would wear three of Li's creations, a total of thirty-six designs. There would be two short breaks in between, for the changing of clothes. The models would walk the runway, representing the change of seasons from spring to summer. The spring line would be shown first. It would begin with men's light coats and jackets. The summer line would follow, with a showing of light jackets, shirts, and trousers. The show would end with a display of summer shorts.

~~~

The sun that had blessed the city during the day was setting, leaving an apricot sky. The full moon was enchanting in the twilight. It shimmered through the tree branches, casting shadows in just the right places. The scene looked like a

Thomas Kinkade masterpiece. As night fell, the moon revealed its brilliance as it ducked in and out from the clouds.

~~~

The family stood at the entrance to Central Park with Chen carrying the food basket. The basket was heavy, so the others offered to take turns carrying it. They chose the Great Lawn, for their picnic, with a view of Belvedere Castle sitting high on a bluff overlooking Turtle Pond.

Chen spread the blanket out on an area of lush green pasture, and the family sat. They ate the hot dogs Chen had promised and drank the bubbly sodas of orange and sarsaparilla. They viewed the buildings, lit up by city lights, and they listened to the music that winded its way through the park lanes. They watched cyclists speed by, as their headlights cast light upon the bike paths lined with trees.

The moonlight shone on parents pushing strollers and baby carriages. Children were still flying kites as they ran across the lush lawns that were blanketed in a light emerald. The moon's brilliance was illuminating life in motion!

~~~

The day of the fashion show arrived. Everyone in the Young family rose early. They showered and dressed and took breakfast in their rooms.

The show was to begin at 11 a.m. Li was all nerves. Hua tried to calm him, but it didn't help.

The family arrived an hour before the show. Li was backstage checking on the models. He made sure every stitch and hem were perfect and every collar straight.

One of the models had popped a button. He offered to pin the opening exposed on his shirt, but Li would have none of it. He wouldn't do it at the Kowloon factory, and he wasn't going to do it here. He had brought a sewing kit with him. To the model's delight it took less than a minute for Li to sew the button back on.

~~~

They say every designer has a theme, or something they wish to convey to their audience. Chen's designs depicted the world of travel, with lightweight spring and summer creations. The destination was America. He was showing his gratitude for the transition he made to a land where he felt your voice counted. A land he would be forever grateful to. The color missing from the fabrics of white and blue Li was able to amplify with accessories of sun glasses, sandals, and men's pebbled leather carryalls, all of a deep Imperial red.

~~~

At 11 a.m. the lights in the tent went on. The tent was packed with spectators, on both sides of the runway. It had opened its white canvas arms to the rich and famous, but also to students who were awarded tickets by their high school teachers as a reward for excelling in Home Economics sewing classes. The students were more excited than those living the life of luxury, in a city that had luxury to offer.

Vincenzo Moncini appeared in the lighted alcove and welcomed the audience. He wore a gray pinstripe suit and a white shirt, but he chose not to wear a tie. His shirt was open at the collar and stayed that way throughout the show. His shoes were the head turner, made of brown two-tone Italian leather. They shined brighter than the overhead floodlights.

"My name is Vincenzo Moncini, of Moncini Originals of Milan," he proudly announced; his amplified voice resonated throughout the tent. The applause thundered under the white canvas. "Today I welcome each of you to the Bryant Park fashion show. I am proud to introduce the spring and summer seasons collection, created by Mr. Li Young our designer. You will get a chance to meet and mingle with the designer after the show."

Whimsical music filled the tent. Moncini waved to the technicians to lower the lights, and the models waited in the wings for the cue to begin their parade.

One by one the models strolled down the catwalk, their ensembles illuminated by the various lights on the runway. The models were poised and balanced as a narrator described each item of clothing in detail. He didn't miss a stitch.

The spring collection had exploded, igniting a burst of applause. A white raincoat opened the show. It had white epaulets on the shoulders and a thick matching belt with a leopard print buckle made of Bakelite. Other designs included a light blue denim jacket with snaps, instead of buttons, and a high collar; a low-waisted black leather jacket that zipped on an angle; and several pullover sweaters. These were followed by lightweight trousers in white, light blue, and navy. This completed the spring collection.

The summer creations were made of light cotton and seersucker. The men's suits had both single and double-breasted jackets. Several jackets were of a silk and cotton blend, in a white-on-white print. The trousers were loose fitting, except for the jeans.

Other designs included men's shorts in white, blue, and denim. Some models wore sea fairing hats. A few striped and solid colored evening shirts had white collars and cuffs.

Most of the male models had hair that nearly touched their shoulders, tousled by a light breeze made possible by the technicians behind the curtain. Other models had their hair pulled back in a short ponytail or piled high on the top of their heads.

The last model stepped onto the catwalk to begin the final walk. Li panicked, and he didn't want to follow him. "What are you worried about?" Moncini asked. "I'll be right behind you."

Li relaxed, as he followed the last model down the runway. Vincenzo Moncini, wanting Li to get full credit for his designs, stayed behind. Unaware he was alone Li strutted to the end of the platform, made a turn and returned to the alcove.

Li had refused to wear a suit. He opted for his Sunday dress of trousers and a white starched shirt with an open collar. When he reached the alcove, he turned to the audience and waved.

The audience went wild. Cheers and whistles could be heard in the streets outside the big white tent. The standing ovation lasted for eight minutes. The show was a great success! Another standing ovation followed when Moncini and Li appeared in the alcove together for a final wave.

Li had learned that the art of runway walking also included facial expression, and the sparkling personality of these seasoned professionals came through. Li was delighted. Hua was watching from backstage. *How will he ever get through this day?*

After the show Li was bombarded with people. Hua was at his side. There were questions to be answered, and there were hands to shake.

Li went to each of the models and thanked them for their performance. Not one tripped or fell. With the sophistication of the professionals they were, they had presented his line of clothing.

Vincenzo Moncini approached Li and gave him a big Latin hug. For a moment Li dropped his shyness and beamed for the photographers. It was truly a day to celebrate.

When the excitement of the day died down, Vincenzo Moncini took Li aside and told him he was opening a shop on Fifth Avenue. Calls had started coming in from well-known department stores.

Manufacturers who wanted to create knock offs of the designs wasted no time.

Vincenzo Moncini promised Li that every item of clothing that sold, with his name on it, would be honored with a handsome check.

~~~

The family remained in New York City for another day. They were able to tour the Metropolitan Museum of Art, on 82$^{nd}$ Street. They saw the Frick collection on Madison

Avenue and taxied down to So Ho and Little Italy, enjoying the food and pastries they offered.

In the late afternoon, they crossed over to Canal Street. They visited Chinatown, but it wasn't the Hong Kong that the Young family knew; at least not to them.

~~~

The following day, the family boarded the plane at John F. Kennedy Airport bound for Camwood. The sun greeted them as they returned to the high mountains, the deep meadows that were covered in wildflowers, the crystal clear streams, and the flowing rivers. And they kept all they had seen and heard in their hearts.

## CHAPTER THIRTY-NINE
(The Letter 2002)

Chen Young sat in his study. He opened the top drawer of his desk and pulled out a few sheets of writing paper. The paper had the Church's logo on top. Chen's name as pastor was printed on the right side with the parsonage's address and phone numbers.

The letter was addressed to Mr. and Mrs. Andrew Boylan who Chen and Niki had paid a visit to a few weeks earlier.

Chen chose not to type the letter but to use his own handwriting. He picked up his favorite pen, dated the letter, and began to write. Unsure of what he would say, he would fill the page one line at a time. Chen prayed before he began.


*Dear Mr. and Mrs. Boylan,*

*Thank you for inviting my wife and I into your home recently to discuss the pending results of the DNA test that would determine the identity of the father of Grace Rose Evans.*

*As you know, we have received the results of the DNA test, and the results speak for themselves. It shows that your son, Richard Boylan, is the father of Grace Rose Evans.*

*I am enclosing a copy of the report for your records. My wife and I have no influence in any charges that may be brought forth by the courts; it is entirely theirs to determine punishment if a crime was committed.*

*However, we have spoken to Grace Rose's mother, Marcie, and we have prayed with her. She wants you to know that in the future, if you desire to see your grandchild, or have a relationship with her, you are welcome to do so.*

*Respectfully yours,*
*Reverend Chen Young*

## CHAPTER FORTY
### (The Land of The Orchid Tree)

Summer in Camwood was an array of color. The purple and white crocuses that came with Spring, the golden daffodils, and the fiery tiger lilies had all disappeared. The yellow forsythia bushes, the weeping cherry blossoms, and the Dogwoods, with their deep pink blooms displaying the nail wounds of Christ, were gone too.

It was August 2002. The morning was warm and inviting. Marcie planned to walk down through the meadow behind the parsonage with her daughter and take the woodland path to the stream. She had invited Samuel to go with her. She packed a picnic lunch for three, thinking she would stay through the early afternoon and return to the parsonage before dinner. She wanted to help Niki with the preparations.

Samuel gladly accepted the invitation. "I want to be back before the sun gets too hot," Marcie told him. "I'll bring the lunch. I plan to read, so bring a good book with you," she instructed.

"What should I bring?" Samuel asked.

"You can bring a classic, like Treasure Island, or you can bring a book with a Christian message, like The Chronicles of Narnia," Marcie suggested. "You'll like that one. I've read it many times. If you have any questions I can help you with them," she added. "Check out the library in the parsonage, they're all there."

~~~

Marcie prepared a soft lunch for Grace Rose and two sandwiches, one for Samuel and one for herself. She planned on using the picnic basket Chen had purchased in New York City. She took it down from the shelf and filled the basket with the lunches. She surrounded the food with packs of ice.

The phone in the study rang. Chen and Niki had gone into town to buy supplies for the church. Marcie hurried to the study and picked up the receiver. "Living Word Church," she said in a sing-song voice. The call was from Mrs. Brandywine. She told Marcie her back went out, and she would not be able to attend the church board meeting on Saturday. "I will relay the message to Pastor Chen," Marcie said. "I'm sure you will receive a visit before then." Marcie wrote down the message and returned to the kitchen to finish packing the lunches.

Marcie removed two folding chairs and the folding stroller from the utility closet. She carried them outside and leaned them against the parsonage wall. She returned to the kitchen to wait for Samuel.

Samuel showed up on time and the two walked down toward the stream together.

The meadow behind the parsonage sloped gently into the woodlands, but it would be impossible to bring Grace Rose safely down the slopes in the stroller. Marcie would carry her.

The woodlands beyond the slopes were covered in thick roots that spread themselves horizontally across the soil. Once they reached the woodlands Marcie and Samuel would find their way to the stream.

As Marcie stood above the meadow, she studied the vast space that crossed from east to west. Its grassland, a blanket of green velvet, sloped in several areas. It was covered in an array of perennials, mixed with wildflowers. The wild yellow daylilies, the pink cone flowers, with their red centers, and the color and sweet fragrance of lavender stretched out across the slopes. *It's a multicolored canvas, one that was painted by God Himself.*

On the west side of the meadow was a parcel of land where tall sunflowers, the color of golden custard, were planted. Their long stems bended in the summer breeze while their young blooms seemed say yes to the brilliant sun.

Marcie took it all in. She imagined a large gathering of people coming together in that green space for a family outing. She pictured both sets of grandparents, the Evanses and the Boylans, picking up Grace Rose and lifting her up and down, her daughter laughing with the sound only a child's giggles can radiate. She saw them picking wildflowers with her. She pictured them throwing a ball and watching her catch it. *Pipe dreams!* Absent from the scene was the father of Grace Rose.

Marcie's warm image faded and another took its place. One of her being stopped from screaming out for help, her small frame being jostled—no, forced to the floor in a dirty closet and overpowered. At the sound of the bell, the students' footfalls reverberated through the hallways. She could hear her cries being stifled with the vibration of hundreds of footsteps changing classes. That image also evaporated in the summer air.

Marcie had purchased a child carrier, and Samuel helped secure it to her back. He gently lifted the infant and strapped her into its seat. Marcie carried the lunch basket, slipping its handles through one arm as she pushed the folding stroller down the slopes with her other hand. She followed Samuel as he descended the incline, carrying the two folding chairs with him.

The picnickers passed the hemlocks with Grace Rose in tow, enjoying the soft summer breeze and the telling scent of sweet pine. The sun shifted and grew warmer as they walked over the bumpy terrain, but the closer they got to the stream the cooler it felt.

The outstretched stream was wide. Its ripples of crystal-clear water created a welcomed mist that caressed their faces. A refreshing gift as the day grew hotter.

When they reached their destination, Samuel asked Marcie if he could remove his shoes and socks to dip his feet. "I don't see why not," she responded. "Go ahead, Samuel, it will feel good."

Samuel walked to the edge of the stream. He removed his shoes and socks and dipped his bare feet in the water. He swayed his feet from side to side, as if he were testing the temperature.

Samuel remained on the ground for about half an hour. He delighted in the rushing water as it passed swiftly over the uneven stones. A small school of silvery minnows passed over Samuel's feet. He yelled out as he reached for his camera. "Minnows are too fast," Marcie interjected. "We can research them, and I will print out some pictures for you."

Marcie enjoyed watching Samuel. She would look at him from time to time as she read. *The most prestigious spa in Manhattan could not rival the therapy of a running stream.* She smiled.

Marcie gazed over at her sleeping daughter. Grace Rose had her mother's large eyes, and her soft hair was the same shade of brown. She had Marcie's skin tone, that of a fresh ripened peach, and she had a countenance about her that glowed, like the angel when he announced Christ had risen! *She will grow to serve God.*

The perpetual sound of ripples, coming from the stream that was fed daily by the mountains above them; the sound of chirping crickets; the ribbiting of frogs; and the sweet songs of the many birds flying overhead, were the only sounds heard that afternoon.

Marcie gazed back at Samuel. "Next time wear your swim trunks under your clothes," she yelled out. "You could wade a bit."

Grace Rose was sleeping peacefully in the stroller. Marcie and Samuel read for about an hour; the tree branches shielding Grace Rose from the sun's rays.

Along with Grace Rose's lunch, Marcie had packed two chicken salad sandwiches, two bottles of water, two bottles of sarsaparilla soda, two apples and two oranges. Samuel picked up the soda bottle Marcie had opened for him and took a swig. "This is good," Samuel said.

"It's not only good tasting," Marcie replied, "but sarsaparilla is good for your health, it boosts your immune system. That is, if you use the natural properties of the berries and root properly. In other words, Samuel, you can't go drinking twenty sodas a day. There are other ways to take it."

After they finished lunch Marcie confronted Samuel. "Samuel, I have something to ask you."

"Yes?"

"We are going to dedicate Grace Rose after church service on Sunday. I would like you to sponsor her."

"What does that mean?"

"It means," she paused, "you would be like Grace's godfather."

Samuel rose from his chair and clapped his hands. "Hooray," he shouted. So, it was settled! Samuel would hold the infant in his arms on Sunday afternoon and pledge his love for Jesus and his commitment to be part of Grace Rose's life.

~~~

Sunday brought with it a clear sapphire sky and warm temperatures. Chen checked the cool air system in the sanctuary to make sure it was circulating properly. He was happy he did. He hadn't expected the flow of Camwood residents that walked into the church that afternoon. Before long, the sanctuary was overrun with people. There was standing room only. Many congregated outside the doors, in the warm sun.

Chen provided bottled water to those attending the dedication on the church grounds. A few volunteers set up a sound system, so those outside the church could hear the event that was taking place inside.

Many congregants had come to know and love Marcie and Grace Rose since that Sunday when Marcie walked into the church for the first time, over a year ago.

Marcie dressed Grace Rose in a flowing gown of white, with appliqués of white roses sewn into the organza skirt. It took Niki a month, in her spare time, to sew it. She added tiny seed pearls in the center of each flower, and she created an organza coat, with a flowing pink ribbon that tied at the neckline. Grace's infant shoes were white patent leather, and she wore white cotton socks trimmed with lace.

Samuel was dressed in a gray suit, white shirt, and a blue and yellow print tie. It was the first time anyone had seen him in a suit. He looked five years older and two inches taller. He looked like a grown man, and he felt it. He raised his voice as he spoke about Grace Rose and what she meant to him. He called on Jesus to protect her, and he vowed he would always be there for her. Samuel held Grace Rose high with both arms and dedicated her to the Lord. Marcie was at his side. The sanctuary was so quiet the slightest noise could be heard.

Besides Grace Rose's day, it was Samuel's day to shine, and shine he did! There wasn't a dry eye in the crowd of people that attended the service.

Marcie looked around the church during the dedication ceremony, hoping to see her parents seated somewhere or standing with the crowd that spilled into the vestibule. She also thought of the Boylans. *Maybe they had a change of heart? After all, it was announced publicly. They must have read it.* But they did not come.

Marcie had matured a great deal during the past year. Her response was, "Maybe in time!"

~~~

In the months that followed Chen had done some soul searching. His congregation was growing to the extent he would one day need an addition to the church sanctuary. He made a list of volunteers who had helped in the past. He planned on contacting each one. He would ask if they would be willing to help with the extension.

~~~

It was early Thursday morning when Chen received a call from Li and Hua. They requested a meeting with Chen. There was something they wanted to discuss with him and Niki. Chen set a time for one p.m., so Niki would have time to prepare a light lunch. Chen was curious, but he didn't question them. He would wait.

The threat of rain showers hovered over the foothills. In the afternoon the clouds had moved on. The sun sat high in the heavens, a radiant amber globe, blessing the world with its God-given healing powers, assisting nature and keeping the planets in line. *What a few hours will do,* Chen thought.

Li and Hua arrived several minutes before one p.m. Chen led them to the living area and they sat. Niki was preparing lunch and about finished when Chen called her to join them. Marcie had gone to town with Grace Rose to pick up some yarn, hoping to make her daughter a blanket. She would not be present at this meeting. Li and Hua wanted it that way.

"What's this all about?" Chen asked, disappointed they didn't want Marcie present.

"We want to ask you first, before we discuss this any further. It's not like we are keeping something from Marcie. Please hear us out." Li said.

Chen trusted his father's judgment. Niki brought in a lunch of sandwiches on a tray and glasses of homemade lemonade. The dessert could wait. Niki didn't want to miss a moment.

After they ate Li spoke, as Hua looked on. She was shaking her head up and down and giggling, she was almost giddy. "Son, we would like to buy a parcel of your land to build a home for young mothers who have nowhere to go. We cannot in good conscience live our lives selfishly and not share our good fortune with others. My plan, if you agree, is to build a home for unwed mothers, so their babies can live, without the threat of their mothers having to make a decision, one they will regret for the rest of their lives." Li said this in the Cantonese language.

Chen was taken aback. "Dad, I think it's a wonderful idea." He glanced at his wife. Niki did not understand all that was being said, but she was dabbing her eyes with her handkerchief. Chen translated it all to her.

"You understand, Dad, we have to go through the proper channels to build on this property. There are zoning laws. I know of a surveyor in town. Perhaps I'll stop by in the morning. I'll ask what he can do for us. Is that okay with you?"

"It's more than okay," Li cried. "Your mother and I have been blessed with my designs, but we are still the same mom and dad you have always known. We want to enjoy where we live and the nature around us. We want our fortune to bless others and save lives. We are God's children, and He supplies us with everything we need."

"Like the Shunammite woman?" Chen smiled.

"Yes, that's it! Like the Shunammite woman."

"I'm proud of you both," Chen responded. "What do you want to call this home you are envisioning?"

"We want to call it Marcie's House."

Chen understood why his father wanted to wait. *Once everything is approved, we will tell Marcie.*

~~~

The following morning, Chen took a ride into town. He parked the car in a parking zone that would give him plenty of time to ask the questions he needed to. He stepped into the local building department.

The man situated behind the desk welcomed him. "Hello Reverend, what can I do for you today?"

Chen extended his hand. "Good morning, Stephen. I want to arrange for a surveyor to come and check out the property surrounding my church. There is plenty of acreage I have no intention of using. I am thinking of building a home there. I need to know exactly what I have to do. I need to know the zoning laws and the electrical and plumbing needs for the project, and I need to know if I can use the well that's on the land, instead of using the utility company in town. Whichever would be more economical."

"We can arrange this for you, Reverend Young. I have some information that will tell you everything you need to know, in order to begin the project. If I were you, I'd take one task at a time, starting with the surveying of your land. I can have someone out there tomorrow if you like, and you can start from there."

Chen shook Stephen's hand and thanked him. He returned to the car and drove to his parent's cottage to give them the good news. Their project was underway.

~~~

In the weeks that followed, Chen had received calls from Hong Kong. Old buddies from his school days confided in him; things were changing. Since the island had been given back to China, they were fearful restrictions would be put on their freedom of worship. They were Christian brothers, some with aspirations of going into the ministry.

Chen understood. His emotions were pulling in one direction—to convince his friends to migrate to the United States, but he knew it would not make the situation in Hong Kong any better.

~~~

The coming months were torturous for Chen. One evening, while all was quiet, he called Niki down to his study.

Niki appeared in the doorway. She had ended a phone conversation with Chen's parents, and she was smiling. "What's up?" Niki asked. She pulled a chair closer.

"Niki, I've been praying," Chen leaned toward his wife, "praying hard."

Niki's brow wrinkled. "What about," she asked.

"I've been receiving calls from my Christian friends in Hong Kong. They are troubled and rightfully so. Since Hong Kong has lost its sovereignty, there's a great fear they will lose their religious freedom. These things happen slowly until there is no freedom left. I've been fighting the Lord from all angles, and He has told me I'm to go back—we are to go back, and we are to start a church in Hong Kong. It won't be forever. Maybe a year or two."

"Then what?" Niki asked.

"If we can train a few men to pastor a church of their own, in time the movement will grow. Isn't that how Christianity started?" Chen paused. When there was no response, he continued. "I am going to advertise for a new pastor to take over our church until we return."

"What about Marcie and Grace Rose?" Niki asked. "What about your parents?"

"We can give Marcie the option of coming with us, or she can stay with mom and dad here. I doubt she'll want to leave. She will be a great help to them with Marcie's House, if the zoning is approved, and she will be a great help to the new pastor. Mom and dad can rent the cottage and move into the parsonage for a time. I'm sure they'll agree. What do you say, Nik?"

Chen expected Niki to think about it for a few weeks. To his surprise, she agreed. "Prophecy is being fulfilled every day," Niki responded. "I agree, we can't waste time. We need to reach as many people as we can, like Noah had hoped to do. Unfortunately, that didn't happen. No one but his family entered the ark."

Niki stood and raised her voice an octave, "Chen, we can't let that happen. Every soul is precious in God's sight."

Chen stepped around his desk and embraced his wife. "We will tell the family after I find the right person to take over the Church."

Chen had enough people to help his parents with the plans for Marcie's house. They were all professionals. They would see the construction plans were carried out to his parents' specifications and the setting up of the house organized. They would also be able to help with the extension on the Church, should Chen be delayed. "I'll only be a phone call away!" Chen assured them.

~~~

The following week, Chen placed an ad in the Camwood Daily Gazette for a new pastor. It took nearly a week before any responses came. There were several, but one in particular caught Chen's eye. It was from a man, newly ordained, who had attended the same school of divinity Chen had attended. "I'll arrange a meeting this week. He can learn, as I did, day by day," Chen told Niki.

Chen knew that a great preacher did not have to have high credentials or lots of experience. If he loved the Lord and had a calling, the Holy Spirit would speak for him. After all, most of the apostles, as well as Jesus' disciples, were ordinary men: fishermen, a tax collector, a zealot, and a tentmaker. No degrees here! Yet, the gospel went out to all nations as a result of their ministries. It was God ordained.

~~~

The interview went as planned, and Chen felt confident in his choice of a new pastor. He was at peace.

The Youngs picked the following Sunday, after the service, to discuss their decision to return to Hong Kong. His parents were in agreement. They knew what was happening in Hong Kong, and they wanted to see change there. Marcie also agreed, but declined the option of moving Grace Rose to the island. She would stay behind and help Li and Hua with the parsonage and continue being a good friend to Samuel. She would assist the new pastor as much as possible. She would help to run the office; She would answer phones, print out bulletins, and keep the files in order.

All arrangements for the trip back to Hong Kong were completed. Chen and Niki were in the process of packing, and they were ready to face a future in the Far East.

Li and Hua had arrived when Marcie and Grace Rose came barreling through the door laughing. Marcie had told Grace a funny story. The infant continued to giggle, as if she understood. They went to the sofa and sat next to Chen and Niki. With everyone together Chen told of their plans to leave a week from Monday.

~~~

The week flew swiftly. After Sunday service the family went back to the parsonage for lunch. A rain shower had found its way through the town and seemed to have ended up at their front door. The sound on the roof echoed like an old friend who decided to surprise them with a visit. It was comforting.

After lunch, the family gathered in the living room to relax and share whatever was on their minds.

A loud knock on the door startled them. "I'll get it," Chen said. His smile was that of a Cheshire cat's. In less than 30 seconds, he returned with a strange visitor following.

The stranger's gray suit was wet. He shook his umbrella, drops flying in all directions. "It's not working too well, is it?" He laughed.

The man was tall, at least six foot two, with dark hair. He had a deep dimple on his right cheek that graced his face, each time he smiled. He was clean shaven and well dressed in a gray pinstripe suit, a white starched shirt, and a purple and gray tie. His jaw was strong, as was his countenance. Yet, the family sensed something soft underneath. Maybe it was his kind heart. His periwinkle blue eyes glistened, as if he were holding a wonderful secret that only he and God knew. He eyed everyone in the room, taking his time, as if he were investigating each member of the family, not the other way around.

"Why don't you introduce yourself?" Chen asked.

"Hello everyone, I'm Anthony Lo Bianco, but my friends call me Tony. I'm a newly ordained pastor, and I've taken the position offered me by Pastor Young." He paused and studied each face to see their reaction.

His visit was unexpected. Everyone stared back at Tony without expression. They would make their judgement of him after he finished speaking.

Tony noticed Marcie holding her daughter. Her long chestnut hair, interwoven in braids, was the same color as the acorns that cascaded freely each fall from the oaks surrounding the parsonage. Her braids hung above her shoulders. She looked like a child. He studied Marcie's face, a face so youthful, *the child must be her sister,* Tony thought.

"I'm honored to be here." Tony said. "I could never fill Pastor Chen Young's shoes; It would be an impossibility. I will place my shoes next to where he keeps his and hope someday to fill mine."

Tony's humility was endearing to each family member, and he was immediately accepted into the fold.

With the introductions over, Niki excused herself. "I'll go put up the coffee and tea, and I'll bring in some refreshments while you get to know one another."

After several cups of coffee and hours of conversing Rev. Lo Bianco walked over to Marcie. "May I hold the baby," he asked. He picked up Grace Rose and held her in his arms. He looked directly into Marcie's eyes and smiled. "Hello again, I'm Tony—Tony Lo Bianco."

Marcie looked back at him. Her eyes had a twinkle that wasn't there before. She extended her hand and replied, "Hello, I'm Marcie—Marcie Evans, and this is my daughter you are holding—Grace Rose."

~~~

Chen and Niki boarded the Delta Flight at John F. Kennedy Airport, the following Monday morning, destined for Hong Kong. It was scheduled to take off at 7 a.m. The family had risen early and was there to see them off, including the new pastor.

To everyone's surprise, Chief Darrell Dugan came, along with his wife of 20 years and his four teenagers—all girls.

Many hugs followed until the public announcement system came on: "Will all the passengers bound for Hong Kong proceed to the boarding area."

Chen and Niki hugged Marcie and Grace Rose one more time before saying their final goodbyes. Chen picked up Grace Rose and handed her a little stuffed lamb. "This will be a friend to the lamb you already have," he said. He turned toward the new pastor, Tony Lo Bianco, and gave a quick wink. "Take good care of her," Chen's eyes pointed to Marcie.

Tony smiled. "I will, Pastor."

Chen turned to Marcie and smiled. "Happy birthday, Marcie, we'll be sure to celebrate again, when we return."

The last final goodbyes were said, and the family watched as Chen and Niki disappeared into the gatehouse. They were about to embark on a new assignment. Chen's life was where he wished it to be. It was God ordained.

~~~

"Welcome to Delta Airlines," the pilot said, as the couple took their seats in coach. "We hope you enjoy your flight. Please turn off your phones and listen to the instructions the steward will give you. There will be a short film. We are anticipating clear skies with smooth sailing. The flight will be approximately 16 hours, so take off your shoes and make yourself comfortable. Use the pillows provided."

Chen and Niki could hear the jumbo jet's engine revving up. The couple peered out the window and saw the Delta Terminal shrink in size, as the plane taxied the runway.

Chen looked deep into Niki's eyes and smiled. He took her hand and held it tight. He knew that before midnight, when the plane lands in Hong Kong, his life will have come,

FULL CIRCLE!

END

## FOOTNOTES

All Scripture quotations are taken from the New
American Standard Bible, Copyright 1960, 1962,
1963, 1968, 1971, 1972, 1973, 1975, 1977, 1995,
by Lockman Foundation. Used by permission.

Some characteristic descriptions taken from The
Emotion Thesaurus: A Writer's Guide To Character
Expression, by Angels Ackerman & Becca Puglisi.

Date fact-checking taken from McDougal Littell,
WORLD HISTORY, Patterns of Interaction. Atlas by
RAND MCNALLY.

www.ingramcontent.com/pod-product-compliance
Lightning Source LLC
Chambersburg PA
CBHW071151260626
47162CB00003B/1005